THE NIGHT THEY KILLED JOSS

VARRAN

George Bellairs (1902–1982). He was, by day, a Manchester bank manager with close connections to the University of Manchester. He is often referred to as the English Simenon, as his detective stories combine wicked crimes and classic police procedurals, set in quaint villages.

He was born in Lancashire and married Gladys Mabel Roberts in 1930. He was a devoted Francophile and travelled there frequently, writing for English newspapers and magazines and weaving French towns into his fiction.

Bellairs' first mystery, *Littlejohn on Leave* (1941) introduced his series detective, Detective Inspector Thomas Littlejohn. Full of scandal and intrigue, the series peeks inside small towns in the mid twentieth century and Littlejohn is injected with humour, intelligence and compassion.

He died on the Isle of Man in April 1982 just before his eightieth birthday.

Also By George Bellairs

The Case of the Famished Parson
The Case of the Demented Spiv
Corpses in Enderby
Death in High Provence
Death Sends for the Doctor
Murder Makes Mistakes
Bones in the Wilderness
Toll the Bell for Murder
Death in the Fearful Night
Death in the Wasteland
Death of a Shadow
Intruder in the Dark
Death in Desolation
The Night They Killed Joss Varran

THE NIGHT THEY KILLED JOSS VARRAN

VARRAN

GEORGE BELLAIRS

ipso books

This edition published in 2016 by Ipso Books

First published in 1970 in Great Britain by John Gifford Ltd.

Ipso Books is a division of Peters Fraser + Dunlop Ltd

Drury House, 34-43 Russell Street, London WC2B 5HA
Copyright © George Bellairs, 1970
All rights reserved

CONTENTS

CHAPTER I
THE WAITING WOMAN

Crouched in a dead hamlet in the harshest part of the Ballaugh marshes, locally known as the Curraghs, Close Dhoo cottage was a sad little place which none of the changing seasons seemed to cheer. Always the same in all weathers, with its desolate front garden, its barren trees and its tightly closed door, with the paint peeling off it. The small windows with their shabby curtains hid all that went on inside. The roof, once thatched, was now covered in tarred corrugated iron through which the rust of decay was beginning to show.

The place, once a croft, occupied a small patch of poor ground of under an acre parallel with a shabby, unmetalled road leading farther into the marshes, with a barren garden behind littered with rubbish – ashes, tin cans, old iron and shards of pottery, and a long alley down the middle receding into the wilderness. Its boundaries were marked by old struggling hawthorn bushes leaning at an angle from the prevailing wind. The garden was completely neglected but, in Spring, the daffodils, planted by occupants long gone, bloomed in profusion and the fuchsias, as old as the house itself, blossomed unseen.

The locality was hushed and seemed to be listening for something. Once, the inhabitants of the now deserted hamlet had, as evening fell, been able to set their clocks by the whistle of the last train to Ramsey leaving the station two miles away. Now they had all gone, railway and people, except the solitary occupant of the lonely house. She was sitting in a plain wooden armchair beside the dying fire of wood in the primitive hearth, waiting. A small, prematurely aged woman, with a resigned weatherworn face in a frame of straight, grey close-cut hair. The fading light of the late autumn day dimly lit up her face and revealed the tight skin showing the bones of the skull beneath, the small thin mouth and the broad snub nose.

The interior of the house consisted of one large room, with a smaller one leading off it and a lean-to kitchen. In the background, a plank ladder led to a trap-door in the loft. The place with its simple old furniture had a dreary look. Full of memories of a departed family. Isabel Varran, the occupant, was one of a family of ten, all scattered except herself and the brother, Josiah, for whom she was now waiting. The walls of the room were decorated with old fly-blown photographs of children, wedding groups posed among absurd Victorian cardboard scenery, or of individual men and women staring with almost frightened looks at the camera behind which the photographer had counted out the interminable seconds to secure the likeness.

A ramshackle green van drew up at the gate and a hefty fat woman in an old coat and with her hair covered by a soiled gaudy scarf, emerged, wobbled up the path and entered the room without knocking at the door. The wind, the muffled drumming of which was rising, entered with her and blew the low fire into flame and drew puffs of aromatic smoke from the smouldering gorse wood into the room.

The newcomer was too inquisitive even to greet the waiting woman.

'Has Joss come yet?'

She wore old trousers and gumboots and was panting heavily from her efforts. She placed her hands flat on the table and rested her great lumbering body on her powerful arms.

The other slowly raised her head and gave her sister a weary, baffled look.

'No. I don't know what...'

The other cut her off quickly.

'Of course, you know as well as I do. The boat arrived in Douglas from Liverpool hours since. He's stopping at all the pubs on his way here. It's just like him. You'd think after more than twelve months in gaol for drunken violence, he'd have had enough. But our Joss was always too clever to learn...'

She paused to gulp in air.

'I suppose he'll be here after the pubs close. Well, I haven't time to wait. I'm going now. Sydney's been out all day. He says there's a farmers' meeting of some sort in Ramsey, but I don't know what he's up to. I've had all the milking to do. The doctor told me to take things easy. I expect that one day I'll drop down dead and that'll be the end of it.'

And with that depressing prognosis, she left as she had come, without a word of farewell. The rattle of the old van died away in the distance and silence descended again, punctuated by the steady tick-tack of the cheap alarm clock on the dresser.

Left alone, the woman remained in her chair, lost in her own thoughts, her hands together in her lap as if in prayer, except that she monotonously rotated her thumbs round one another, a habit which had been her mother's, too, when she was anxious about anything. As the last of the sad daylight faded from the room, she rose and switched on the solitary electric light which hung over the table, a single lamp in a cheap pink shade. The lamp illuminated the room more starkly than the struggling daylight and revealed the well-polished Welsh dresser, the oak corner cupboard and the worn rush-bottomed chairs.

She went again to the door, looked out and then shone a torch into the darkness. A damp smell of trees and earth from the garden entered the room. She closed the door again with an anxious forlorn gesture and went to the kitchen and filled an electric kettle and made some tea. Then she cut thick slices of bread and butter, produced some cold cooked sausages from the pantry and set out her meal on one corner of the table under the light in the living-room. She ate her meal, slowly masticating it and washing it down with draughts of tea from a large mug. She seemed lost in thought and took no interest in what she was doing. Only once did she show any sign of where her thoughts were wandering. Half-way through her feeding, she rose, paused and then went to the sideboard and took out a purse, from which she counted twenty one pound notes. She replaced three of these and with the rest in one hand, groped up the chimney of the wide hearth and with the other brought down an old metal teapot. She stuffed the money in it and replaced it. Just in case her brother indulged in his old habit of helping himself to her savings. Then she finished her tea. Twice more in the course of tidying and washing-up she went to the door and looked out into the night. There was nobody about. In the distance a dog barked and far away the headlamps of a passing car shone across the marshes, from which a thin mist was rising, and faded away. She put on a pair of spectacles and sat again in the chair by the fire, which she revived with wood from a box on the hearth, and began to read a book she had borrowed from the country library. Soon she had fallen asleep.

She moved and the book falling from her lap awakened her. She sat up with a start and looked at the clock. Five minutes past ten. She rose in a flurry and hurried to the door, gathering up the torch on her way. Outside it was pitch dark. The wind had dropped and now hissed quietly in the bushes along the road. The woman stood at the door, the light from her torch illuminating the path and the ramshackle wooden gate. She remained there for a minute, lost in thought, wondering when her brother would finally turn up. Then, almost mechanically, she moved into the dark and walked to the gate, struggled briefly with the broken catch and stepped out into the road. She shone her torch here and there and suddenly brought the beam to rest on a huddled bundle under the hedge opposite the house. She hurried across and stooped over it.

For one incredulous minute she examined what she had found and then uttered a shrill wail. It was the body of a man.

The corpse lay face downwards with arms spread above its head. All around the earth was disturbed, as though there had been a struggle or the murderer had tried to drag him further into the bushes. There was no doubt about the cause of death. There was a gaping wound in the back of the head and a streak of congealed blood running from the skull and round one side of the neck.

The woman stood for a moment panting and whimpering. The flashlight, which was almost played-out and now gave forth a faint red glimmer, fell from her hands. She did not trouble to rescue it, but first ran along the path to the house, illuminated by the light shining through the doorway, and then back to the road and vanished in the darkness.

Even in the dark, the woman knew her way about. As soon as she stepped off the rambling highway of two barely discernible tracks almost obliterated by grass and weeds, a labyrinth of corkscrew paths overhung by marsh shrubs and trees spread in every direction. Without hesitating, she made her way through the wilderness, running and then reducing her speed to a walk as she recovered her breath. Finally, she emerged on a narrow macadamed road. Almost at the junction stood a whitewashed farmstead in a large yard. Before she reached it a dog emerged boiling from his kennel, came to the end of his tether, and hurled himself savagely on his hind legs struggling to get free. As the woman entered the farmyard, a window in the house opened and a man's voice cursed the dog and yelled at him to be quiet.

Above the noise of the man and dog, the woman tried to make herself heard.

'Joss is dead. Somebody's killed him.'

The man at the window leaned out farther, peering into the dark. Suddenly wakened from his first sleep, he was bemused and he half wondered if in the confusion of its furious barking, the dog had started to articulate as well. He shouted back into the blackness.

'What do you say?'

The woman screamed this time at the top of her voice.

'Joss has been killed!'

Without another word the head above vanished and the window was slammed. A light went on in the room and was followed by one after another from other windows as the occupants awoke there. Finally, the general turmoil inside seemed to rouse the occupant of a tower erected at one end of the house and the light went on there, too, and joined the rest of the illuminations.

The woman stood motionless and dazed. Now and then she whimpered in protest at the time the occupants were taking to appear.

Suddenly the door opened and a shaft of light shot across the neat path to the large white gate and the forlorn figure of the woman waiting like a ghost near the house.

Silhouetted in the doorway stood a fat, stocky, middle-aged man in pyjama top and trousers with his braces dangling behind him like a tail. He had close-cropped hair, a stubble of iron-grey beard, large ears and a strong short neck. He rubbed the sleep from his eyes.

'Who is it?'

'Isabel Varran from Close Dhoo. Joss has been killed.'

The man grunted.

The family at Close-e-Cass scarcely knew their nearest neighbours. The Varrans were reputed to be a queer lot and Isabel was regarded as being the oddest of them.

'What did you say about Joss?'

'He's dead. Somebody killed him.'

'Where is he?'

'In the hedge opposite our house.'

'Are you sure he's dead?'

Meanwhile other members of the family had gathered round the fat man. Three men, one of whom might have been his brother and the others his sons. Joseph Candell, the fat man, didn't seem at all pleased by the disturbance and his involvement in it. He was a man of little initiative and hesitated about his next move. Meanwhile, the dog began to bark again. It gave him a chance to vent his feelings and he ran to the kennel and kicked the dog, which ran yelping for shelter.

A bell, dangling from a spring on the wall of the hall began to jangle. It was from the occupant of the strange tower, who rarely left it, and called for attention by the home-made alarm.

An elderly woman appeared, her grey hair in rollers, with a coat over her nightdress.

'What's going on here? Grandfather's getting up.'

'Go and tell him to keep out of this and be quiet.'

The woman, Candell's wife, didn't seem to hear but passed him and went to the solitary figure waiting in the dark for the next move.

'What is it, Isabel?'

At the sound of the gentle voice of the older woman, the younger one suddenly burst into noisy weeping.

'Joss is dead…'

'Come indoors out of the cold.'

She laid her hand on Isabel's shoulder and led her inside. As she passed the group of men she turned on them.

'Well, what are you lot waiting for? Get along with you to Close Dhoo and see what's been happening there. I'll make some tea for her. She can wait here.'

A figure then appeared on the landing of the wide staircase. A fierce-looking old man with a flurry of shaggy white hair, tall and stooping, dressed in a calf-length white nightshirt. It was old Junius Candell, aged about ninety, who years ago had surrendered the running of the farm and a small share of the capital and profits to his eldest son and retired to a tower which he had built on the end of the house. He spent most of his time there watching all that went on in all the fields and buildings.

'What's the hullaballo about? Nobody tells me anything.'

Old Junius waved his stick in the air. It had, in days past, been laid so often across his son's back, that the fat man at the door made an instinctive gesture with his left arm as though to ward off a blow.

The last arrival on the stairs was the fat man's daughter. She was dressed in a negligée, bought from a mail order firm and certified 'as worn by famous actresses'. She was pretty and had slant eyes, which made her father sometimes doubt his paternity and jealously dream-up affairs long gone between his wife and proprietors of Chinese restaurants, which seemed to be the only places on the Isle of Man which harboured orientals.

Mrs. Candell appeared to be the only person with any initiative. She turned on the two younger men.

'Get back to your room and get dressed. Somebody will have to go down to Close Dhoo and see what this is about.'

Then she addressed the slant-eyed girl, who was leaning against the wall half-way up the stairs, breathing on her finger nails and rubbing them on the sleeve of her *peignoir*, as the advertisement had called it.

'And you, Beulah, have you nothing better to do? See your grandfather back to his room. He'll be getting his death of cold. Tell him to get in bed.'

The old man gave the girl a toothless grin as she approached him. She was obviously the apple of his eye.

'Come on, grandad. She says you're to get back to bed.'

'Eh?'

He was a bit deaf. She led him away.

The clock in the hall struck midnight. The men, who had scattered when Mrs. Candell told them to go and dress now gathered again at the door. The two sons, tall, heavy, slow moving, looked to their father for his orders. The fat man seemed to realise at last that they had better do something quickly, put on his cap and took a large stick from a collection of many generations in an umbrella stand near the front door.

'We'd better three of us go. Uncle Tom, stay with the women. We don't know who's prowling about. If what the Varran girl says is true, we ought to get the police ... '

The younger of the sons, in his early twenties, with a beatnik haircut and sideboards, giggled nervously.

'We ought to be sure she's tellin' the truth, oughtn't we? If Bella Varran has imagined it all, we'll look daft when the police get here and find it's nothing but a hoax ... '

'You shut up! If we leave a dead man lying in the ditch all night, we'll be in proper trouble.'

The older son, a smiling, naïve, good-tempered giant, thought he ought to say a word.

'Had I better take me gun?'

The fat man was out of patience with the whole business and wanted to get back to bed.

'What the hell would we want with a gun? Whoever's done this, if it has been done, will be miles off by now. Let's get goin'. Bring the big flashlamp ... '

The fat man walked very fast and with the assurance of one who knew every step of the way. The air was still and cold and the quick clatter of the men's hobnailed boots against the loose flints of the track made them sound like a group of horses. At first, nobody spoke. The fat man breathed asthmatically through his mouth. He was still half-drunk with sleep and grumbling to himself about the ruin of his night's rest. The youngest son was talking quietly, pursuing his original train of thought.

'A lot of fine fools we'll look if ... '

'Shut up and save your breath!'

Nobody knew what Joseph Candell was thinking about. Nobody ever did. He was a lumbering, slow thinking man who spoke little, had difficulty in expressing himself and grew irritable when he could not do so. Now, the pace was too fast for him. He began to wonder why he was hurrying and slackened his steps. His sons followed suit and the younger one paused to light a cigarette. They had reached the long twisting path which led to Close Dhoo and left behind the tunnel of trees which had once been planted as a part of the scheme when the great trench was dug to drain the marshes. As they reached the wider track, above which the stars were now visible, the sky seemed to pale in the direction of Ballaugh, giving an illusion that dawn was near.

A light shone out from a solitary cottage ahead of them.

'There's Close Dhoo. She must have left the light on.'

Nobody answered, but they all thought alike. Descended from a race of peasants, all waste was abhorrent to them. The three men reduced their pace, as though reluctant to face what was awaiting them. They felt like intruders in a matter which did not concern them.

The younger son, his hands in his pockets, had been whistling nervously between his teeth.

'What do we do when we get there?'

The fat man, faced with a decision, grew irritable, as usual.

'What the hell do you think we'll do? She said his body was in the ditch opposite the house. You and Baz can go and look for it. I'll go and see what's going on in the house.'

They reached the house and paused irresolutely. In the silence they could hear water babbling somewhere.

'Well? What are you two waiting for? Get on with it.'

The two Candell boys obeyed. Their nailed boots clattered across the flints and then fell silent as they met the soft mould of the hedge. Their father strode boldly up the path of trodden earth to the front door. Before entering he peeped through the window at the side, but the curtains obscured all that was within. He hesitated before trying the door and looked back to where his sons had left him. He could not see them, but the noise of crackling twigs and the dancing light of the torch they were carrying indicated that they were vigorously tackling the job in hand.

'Hey!'

The shrill shout breaking the silence pulled them up. Their father hurried down the path and found them knee-deep in the ditch.

'There's nobody here. I said she'd imagined it and we'd be made to look fools...'

'Shut up! And what do you think you're doing there? If you find the dead man and the police are brought in, there'll be a hell of a row because you've trampled all over the place and spoiled the clues with your big feet...'

'Fine fools we look...'

'Shut up, I said. We ought never to have started searching for the body. And it's me who is the fool turning the pair of you loose on the job. I might have known you'd mess it up.'

He paused and blew through his mouth.

'There's only one thing for it. We'd better get the police. We can't run the risk of interfering any more. It's their responsibility. Put that light out and come back to the road...'

The three of them scrambled out of the mud and peat of the ditch and stood in the road hesitantly.

'It's as near to the village as going back home to telephone. Baz, you'd better walk down and get the policeman. I've had enough of this. Somebody else had better take the responsibility. As it is, there'll be trouble when they find how the pair of you have trampled all over the place.'

'It's a good half hour's walk from here...'

'Don't argue with me. I'd send Joe, only he won't be able to tell a proper tale. As it is, I'm sure you'll make a mess of it, too. Just go and knock up Kincaid and tell him that Isabel Varran has come and told us that she's found her brother Joss dead in the road, and he'd better come right away. Got that? Nothing else. Don't start spinning a long yarn. I know what you're like when you get talking. So watch your tongue if you don't want trouble. Bring Kincaid here. We'll wait in the house.'

Baz was too bewildered even to argue and went off in the darkness. His hobnails rang on the road and gradually receded until there was silence again.

'We'd better go in and wait. No sense in standing out here in the dark.'

They crossed the road and down the path to the house. Candell was first and fumbled with the latch.

'What the ... ?'

He pushed open the door and in the shaft of light from the room looked at his podgy hand.

It was covered in dark congealed blood.

He hurried indoors and his son shambled after him.

The room was as neat and tidy as Isabel Varran had left it. The table was covered with a red velvet cloth and in the middle stood a half-empty bottle of whisky without a cork.

The centre of the stage, however, was occupied by a solitary figure slumped in an arm-chair before the dead fire. The head lay on one side in an attitude of great weariness and the arms dangled one each over the arms of the chair, the hands outstretched and the soiled broken fingernails almost touching the floor.

The features were those of a man of middle age, lined and grubby, and with several days' growth of beard. The square head, with its thatch of close-cropped iron-grey hair, was thrown back and the eyes were open and staring. He wore an old suit and soiled shirt without tie. The shirt front was soaked in whisky, the reek of which filled the room, as though someone had tried to revive him by forcing it between his teeth.

The younger man stared wild-eyed at the body, his lips moving soundlessly. Then he ran out into the garden and his father could hear him retching.

The older man approached the corpse, his fat arms ahead of him, like someone forcing his way through a thick hedge. He touched the cold forehead with the flat of his hand, uttered a noise like a sob and then, with a quick gesture, closed the staring eyes with his forefinger and thumb. Then he ran to join his son outside.

Half an hour later when Baz and the village constable arrived in the latter's official car, they found the fat man and Joe sitting on the doorstep with the door locked behind them, staring into space.

CHAPTER II
DEAD MAN'S DOSSIER

It was evening when Inspector Knell, of the Isle of Man police, in charge of the Close Dhoo case, finished his enquiries on the spot. He had been hard at work all day, and, as he left the dead man's house, he drove to the main highway through Ballaugh village, along the road skirting the central hills and through the silent valley to Grenaby parsonage.

Chief Superintendent Littlejohn, of Scotland Yard, had arrived at the vicarage there, the home of his friend the Archdeacon of Man, late that afternoon. Early in the day, the Manx police had telephoned Scotland Yard for information about the murdered man, who had just been released from Wormwood Scrubs prison after serving a sentence for attacking a sailor with a broken bottle in a drunken brawl in Limehouse. Any opportunity of visiting the Isle of Man was pleasing to Littlejohn and he had had as much information as possible collected and had brought the file in person.

Knell, as usual, received a frosty welcome from Maggie Keggin, the Archdeacon's housekeeper.

'So, it's you again. You're a nuisance. When you call here it's either because the supper is just on the table or else there's been a murther. What is it this time?'

She was Knell's second cousin and, as one of the family, could speak her mind without reserve whilst resenting any criticism by outsiders.

Knell bared his large teeth in a friendly grin.

'I called to pay my respects to the Chief Superintendent and, of course, to you as well, Maggie. Has he arrived?'

'He got here less than an hour ago and here you are, botherin' him before he's even had time to unpack his bag. It's another murther, isn't it? I can tell by the way you're avoiding giving me an honest answer...'

The argument was interrupted by the arrival of the Venerable Archdeacon in the hall.

'What's all this chatter about? Who is it?'

The old man cut a fine figure, with his froth of white beard, his old-fashioned cut of ecclesiastical clothes including gaiters, and the red leather house-slippers on his feet which gave a final splash of colour to his clerical black.

'Oh, it's you, Reginald. Come inside. You're quick to follow the bad news...'

'I knew it! He's like Berry Dhone, the witch, trailing the bad luck about with him. There isn't enough supper cooked for him, so he can go hungry as he intrudes on Inspector Littlejohn.'

'Chief Superintendent, Maggie. How often have we to tell you?'

Maggie Keggin's lips tightened to a thin line. She refused to admit that a Superintendent in any walk of life stood higher than an Inspector and persisted in giving Littlejohn the rank he had carried when first she met him years ago.

They went indoors.

Littlejohn was standing at the window watching the last light of the day vanishing behind the hills. In such surrounding, talk of murder seemed like brawling in church.

'Hullo, Knell!'

Maggie Keggin would have been more pleased if Littlejohn had received Knell in an off-hand manner for disturbing his peace, but as the pair of them seemed delighted to meet again, she relented, and laid a third place at table.

'It's pheasant and a good job it's a big one. And I'm just going to serve it, so don't you start discussing murthers, Reginal Knell, till I've cleared up after the meal. Eat and enjoy your food without adding the sauce of horrors to it, and thank the good God for his bounty.'

She did not add that the bounty had been provided through a well-known local poacher, who, to keep his luck alive, now and then, unknown to the Archdeacon, gave a portion of his spoils to the church through the vicarage back door.

It was not until the remnants of the meal had been cleared and the port placed on the table that the three men began to discuss the crime. Maggie Keggin left them to their own devices and went to enjoy her private television.

'We'll not be disturbed until bedtime,' commented the Archdeacon. 'There's a boxing match on tonight. Maggie watches them all. One of her family was a famous boxer years ago ... '

'Jimmy Cregeen.'

'I'd forgotten he was also a relative of yours, Reginald. Want to join Maggie in her sitting-room?'

Knell's face assumed a faint expression which for lack of anything better would have been a smile.

'Shall we get on with the Close Dhoo affair, Archdeacon?'

Littlejohn produced a thin file which he had brought with him and Knell took out the leather-bound notebook which he used on special cases and which his eldest daughter had bought for him last Christmas. Littlejohn indicated that Knell had better speak first and lit his pipe.

Knell's account assumed the nature of a lecture. He had been busy in the Close Dhoo neighbourhood from the small hours of the day almost until dusk and had accumulated a lot of information. Now and then, as he refreshed himself from his notebook, his face assumed a puzzled expression, for in the excitement of the enquiry he had written at great speed and in places couldn't read his own writing.

'I was wakened early this morning ... three-thirty, to be precise ... by headquarters who said the constable at Ballaugh had reported a murder in the curraghs at a place called Close Dhoo. If I might have a map, I'll show you exactly where the place is ... '

The Archdeacon not only produced the map, but opened it and placed his finger on the spot without hesitation.

'Close Dhoo,' he said, 'means Black Enclosure. The Manx word "Close" usually refers to a croft or small holding. 'Dhoo', or black, is not as ominous as one might think. It probably refers to the nature of the soil or the colour of the peat on the land. The Chief Superintendent tells me that Joss Varran was the victim of the crime. Do you know the background of that family?'

'Not very well, sir. We've been concerned with the details of the murder all day.'

'Mind if I intrude with some information?'

'Not at all. It would be very helpful.'

'Years ago, when I was a young curate, I deputised for the vicar of Ballaugh whom illness kept from his duties for six months and I became familiar with that neighbourhood. I was, for a time, very occupied with Close Dhoo, because during my stay in Ballaugh it became the centre of a rumpus in which I had to arbitrate.'

He paused to refill the glasses with port.

'In those days, it had ceased to be worked as a croft and had been used as a tied cottage for labourers at the neighbouring farm of Close-e-Cass, which has been occupied by the Candells for generations; another Close which in course of time has grown into a large and prosperous farm by the buying-in of neighbouring holdings.'

'It was the Candells who informed the police of the murder, sir. When his sister found Joss's body, she went to Close-e-Cass and roused them.'

'Close Dhoo was empty in the days when I arrived in Ballaugh and, I imagine, although I haven't seen it for many years, it is still in the ramshackle state in which I found it then. Briefly, it was, as I say, empty, and the trouble arose because Michael Varran, the father of the murdered man, brought his family there and squatted in the house. I don't know where he came from. It was said, at the time, that he came from the south of the Island. That may have been so; but it is the custom, as you know, for the northern folk to try to prove all the local reprobates are of southern origins and the southern folk to return the compliment about all the rascals of their parts. Mike Varran brought his wife and two children, and another on the way, and settled in Close Dhoo.'

The discourse was then interrupted by a wild hullabaloo from the room across the passage where presumably Maggie Keggin's boxing match was heating-up.

'The Candells, who owned it, were, and still are, a wealthy prosperous lot and, of course, resisted the intrusion of the Varrans. They tried to evict them and there were fisticuffs. Mike Varran was a shiftless type, but his wife was hardworking and decent and naturally, as she had two small children and was again pregnant, local sympathy was on her side. I was asked to arbitrate and try to come to some arrangement with the Candells. It was difficult, for they were a stubborn family, but I finally managed to arrange a small rent for the place, arguing that it was in poor condition and likely to tumble down unless cared for by somebody, for example, a tenant. The Varrans had a pretty thin time, but, largely owing to the mother's efforts, I think they kept up with the rent. I believe Joss Varran eventually bought the place for a song. They were a large family...'

Knell consulted his notebook.

'I'm told there were ten children...'

'Yes; I'd an idea that was the case.'

'I got a list of the survivors from Isabel Varran. There are only five of them left.'

'I know several died in childhood. There was a lot of infant mortality in those days. Even five of them with their parents must have lived like peas in a pod in that little place. Damp, ill-nourished... and with consumption running in families, it's a wonder so many of them survived.'

'Of the five remaining, Joss, Isabel and Rose, who married a farmer called Handy at Narradale, were living on the Isle of Man. The other two, Bennie and Nessie, married and emigrated, one to Canada and the other to Australia. Isabel is regarded as a bit queer. Who wouldn't be, living, for the most part, all alone in that lonely cottage in a spooky part of the marshes? There isn't even a decent road to it. Only a rutted lane. Her only regular visitor is her sister, Rose. Her only near neighbours are the Candells, who won't have any truck with her. That's largely due to Joss, who's spent several spells in gaol and is a bit of a local outcast. The Candells hadn't seen Isabel for years until she turned up asking for help. Mrs. Candell has been very decent to her and she stayed with them at Close-e-Cass last night.'

Littlejohn opened the file at his elbow.

'Have you tried to check Joss Varran's movements since he left gaol, Knell?'

'Our men have been working all day gathering what information they could. Our results are a bit scattered and begin at Liverpool, where he caught the morning boat home. That was yesterday. One of the sailors on the boat recognised him and spoke to him. Joss was a surly sort and the sailor got nothing from him. He did, however, spend a lot of time in the bar, drinking, and then he left the boat immediately she docked in Douglas. There we lost his tracks. We have a photograph of him in our records. He's been in prison a time or two here. Our men enquired at most of the pubs in the centre of the town, but nobody had seen him. Nor had any of the bus or electric railway staff. He must have thumbed a lift from Douglas to Ramsey, because he turned up at the "Eagle and Child", Ramsey at about 5 o'clock. The landlord there remembered him. Joss was as sulky as usual and little conversation passed between them. The landlord said the encounter was a bit embarrassing with Joss just having come out of prison and he didn't know what to say to him. After a couple of drinks, Joss left. That would be about half-past five. From then onwards, we find no trace of him. He may have walked home, or begged a lift. We're enquiring about that. So far, we've drawn a blank on all his movements...'

Littlejohn passed over his file.

'Between hearing from you at nine this morning and my taking the afternoon plane, I managed to get a little about Varran. You'll have some of the information on your own files, but from our records you'll see he was a deck hand on a cargo boat before he was gaoled. The *Mary Peters*, registered at Preston. He and some of his mates got drunk in

Limehouse and Varran got in a fight and went for a man with a broken bottle. His two companions got light sentences for being drunk and disorderly, but he got two years, because in addition to his offence, he had a previous record. He seems to have been a violent man and was birched at the age of eighteen for criminal assault in Ramsey. After that, he served short terms for petty larceny and drunk and disorderly conduct.'

'I see he got remission for good conduct.'

'Yes. He behaved himself, but was surly, as may be expected. He left the Scrubs at nine in the morning of the day before his arrival in Douglas. He told the warder at the prison gate that he was going home on the next available boat, which he did, apparently. We don't know where he stayed overnight.'

'I see you enquired about any friends he may have made whilst inside.'

'He appears to have been far from friendly and confiding, but for most of his term he shared a cell with two men, a safebreaker called John Jukes, otherwise Cracker Jack, and a housebreaker named Cliff Larkin. Both men were released a week or two before Varran. We've still to trace them and enquire if Joss had anything interesting to say to them about his programme when he got out.'

'You think that perhaps he was killed for something he did before he was gaoled?'

'That may easily be the case.'

'Was he alone when he left the Scrubs?'

'Yes. The man at the gate was sure of that. Are you thinking that someone was waiting there for him intent on killing him?'

'Yes, sir. It may have been someone connected with the man he damaged in the fight, or even the man himself.

He might not have wished to kill him, but just beat him up for what he'd done. Because the police surgeon's report is rather strange. Death was due to brain damage caused by a blow on the head, but previous to that, Joss had been badly knocked about. There were bruises on the face and some on the body which might have been caused by someone putting in the boot.'

'Perhaps the man following him couldn't get Joss to himself and then got an opportunity after he left Ramsey. Could Joss have been beaten up and then staggered home to die on the doorstep?'

'If I give you full details of how Joss was found, you'll see it's more intricate than that. Isabel, his sister, says she found him in the hedge across the track from the house. She swears he was dead then, although that's only her idea. She'd no way of knowing, except that he *looked* dead. He might have been unconscious. The doctor says that he died somewhere about the time when she found him. Without more ado, Isabel ran to the Candells' place and roused them. Three of the men, father and two sons, hurried to Close Dhoo and there found the body of Joss in an arm-chair inside the house. He was dead. But there was a bottle of whisky on the table and the front of the body was soaked in whisky, too. It looks as if there might have been a struggle opposite the house. There are marks which might have been made in a scuffle in the ditch there, but the Candell boys got so enthusiastic hunting for Varran's body, that they've ruined any useful footprints or other traces. Whoever attacked Joss must have been disturbed by Isabel and hid in the hedge. Then, after she left for help, he carried Joss's body to the house and tried to revive him. Finding him dead, he went off in a hurry.'

'Fingerprints?'

'None on the bottle or on the furniture, as far as we could see. Whoever did it was sharp enough to wipe them clean.'

'Anybody who watches television knows the technique. It doesn't need brains nowadays; it's mere routine.'

'That's as far as we've got, for the present. It looks like being a long hard haul before we find out who's responsible for last night's events.'

'Did Varran let his sister know beforehand that he was coming home, and when?'

'No. He didn't write to say when Isabel could expect him. She said she had an idea about when he'd be released, but nothing definite. Her sister, Rose, asked the vicar if he could find out, which he did by telephoning the prison chaplain.'

'Did Joss write to her regularly from gaol?'

'She said not. If he ever wanted anything, he seems to have sent her a peremptory note and asked for it. She wrote to him regularly, but he never replied to her letters and once or twice she suggested she might visit him, but got no answer. A bit rough of him, I must say. Isabel is a shy, awkward sort of woman and such a visit to London would have been a big ordeal. She's never been off the Island in her life and, as far as she's concerned, England might be on the other side of the world.'

'What kind of a reception did you get in the curraghs in the course of your investigation, Knell?'

'I could hardly call it frosty. They are, for the most part, hospitable, kindly folk, but murder is, of course, almost unknown there and an event like this draws them closer together and they get cautious and suspicious. It's as though they're afraid of becoming involved in some way, either by revenge from someone they might betray or by incriminating someone in their family, which, through intermarriage is sure to be widespread and to the members of which they are fanatically loyal in the face of outsiders.'

The Archdeacon intervened.

'I knew the Candell family long ago. They were peasants who elevated themselves by hard work and thrift. And peasants everywhere are sly, cautious and suspicious.'

Knell smiled.

'That's right. But I had what you might call an entrée. I had an uncle who was a preacher in the North of the Island. He used to visit some of the little chapels dotted about the curraghs and district and was well-known and popular. When I mentioned his name the Candells thawed out a bit. Particularly Mrs. Candell who's a woman of character and is more educated and talkative than the men. She told me about the strained relations that had existed between the Varrans and the Candells. She seemed quite relieved that Isabel had come to them for help and that the long feud had apparently come to an end.'

'Feud, did you say, Reginald?'

'You might call it a sort of mental feud, Archdeacon. There was no violence, but every friendly approach the Candells ever made to the Varrans was rudely repulsed until there was almost hatred between them. You admit, sir, that the house was originally rented through your good offices and later the Varrans bought it through a third party.'

'Do you think the Candells might be involved in this crime?'

'Certainly not. There's a decency about all of them and they wouldn't beat up and murder people. That's my opinion, at any rate.'

He looked hopefully at Littlejohn.

'How long are you staying on the Island, sir?'

'If you need an assistant, Knell, I could manage a few days here ... '

Knell rubbed his hands together.

'In that case, would you like to come with me to the curraghs tomorrow?'

'Of course. It's years since I was last there. Wasn't it in the curraghs that we were involved in a case where the parson went off his head and rang the church bells at midnight?'

'That's it, sir. That was a long time ago ... '

Knell said it sadly, as though he wished time would turn back and restore him to the golden years of his prime.

'And what will we do when we get there, Knell?'

'I thought you might like to have a talk with Isabel Varran and the Candells ... '

'You think the answer to the problem might be found there?'

'I can't think so, although they are a strange race of people. As I said, why should any of them wish to kill Joss Varran? They probably all despised him, but that doesn't mean a hatred necessary to kill a man.'

'The murderer might have been a stranger. Someone from Joss Varran's past. Perhaps a shipmate or a prison acquaintance who might have originated from anywhere. In that case the criminal could have got clean away.'

'We followed the usual routine of making full enquiries at the boats and the airport. We were on the nine o'clock boat this morning before she sailed. The crew was the same as when Joss Varran crossed yesterday on his way home. None of them saw him with any companion. He was, it seems, visible most of the time, wandering from bar to bar on the boat and drinking pretty heavily. The chances are that the murderer, if he were an outsider and made off back to the mainland after last night's tragedy, would get the nine o'clock boat or else the first plane to England. There were quite a number of strangers left the island by both ways. What could we do? We questioned the crews and the dock and airport staff and our men are keeping the usual watches on departures, but in a case like this, to detain on suspicion of murder any stranger leaving the island would be quite impossible. It would be silly.'

'Quite right.'

'I've been hard at work on the case since it was reported to me in the early hours of this morning, but the bulk of it has been the dreary formal preliminaries of a case which, from the looks of things, is going to be a very hard nut to crack.'

The Archdeacon, who had been listening drowsily to the conversation was obviously disappointed.

'You're telling us, Reginald, that after a day's work, you are in despair. You haven't even started scientifically on the case, yet. You've simply made a few routine notes in your book...'

'Twenty-five pages, Archdeacon...'

'You must be tired. You'll feel better after a night's sleep. The Chief Superintendent and I will be waiting here for you first thing tomorrow morning. You can then take us to Close Dhoo. Is that agreeable to you, Tom?'

'I suppose so, if Knell can bear with us.'

The door opened and Maggie Keggin appeared, flushed from her evening's entertainment.

'Good night to you all,' she said, and then turning upon Knell, as was her custom, to deliver a parting shot, 'And I hope you've remembered as you drank the Venerable Archdeacon's wine, that you've to drive home in a car. It would be a disgrace to our family and to the constabulary, if tomorrow you appeared in dock for drunken drivin'...'

And she departed with that

Knell tried to look as if he was still as fresh as a daisy, without much success. His friends saw him off from the gate and watched the light of his headlamps gradually vanish in the night.

CHAPTER III
THE MEETING AT CLOSE-E-CASS

Littlejohn, the Archdeacon and Knell arrived at Close Dhoo early the following morning. It was sunny, one of the last days of the spent summer, but the recent tragedy and the ominous silence of the back roads and lanes which led to the house cast gloom over the excursion.

The last part of the journey lay through tunnels of trees with their leaves taking on the tints of autumn along a neglected road almost overgrown with grass and weeds. The fading tracks of wheels were faintly visible, like a scar in the course of healing. Now and then, through gaps in the trees, they saw the bastion of kindly hills which suddenly level out into the northern plain.

Knell seemed to be in a melancholy mood, depressed by the deserted desolation of old dead houses crumbling away and uneasy quiet where once there had been a lively community. As they passed a small tumbledown ruin standing askew on the roadside and apparently now used as a shelter for cattle, he drew his companions' attention to it.

'There was once a little colony of people here, crofters, who earned a livelihood by small fanning and fishing and the women worked the land when the men were away with the herring fleet. That wreck over there was a school. The teacher vanished one night. Nobody knew where she went. It's said she eloped with a travelling tinker... Here's Close Dhoo. I was told in the course of my investigations yesterday that an occupant, before the Varrans settled there, a recluse, hanged himself...'

The Archdeacon grew impatient.

'What's the matter with you, Reginald? You seem in a sad state. How many more mysteries are you going to unearth in the locality? Let us solve the death of Joss Varran first and you can deal with the rest at your leisure.'

Knell pulled up at Close Dhoo and took a large key from his pocket, after pointing out the hedge opposite where the trampled foliage and grass indicated the spot where Varran's sister had found his body.

'The body's in the mortuary at Ramsey,' he said to whom it might concern as he fitted and turned the key in the stiff, heavy lock. The damp, slightly fragrant smell of burnt gorse from the cold fire met them.

Knell stood with his hands on his hips and looked slowly round the room.

'We've been over everything. There were no papers or letters in any of the drawers. We searched in the usual places where the likes of the Varrans keep their valuables, including up the chimney. There we found a biscuit tin with family papers in it: registry deeds for this property in the name of Josiah Varran; birth, marriage and death certificates and the like. Nothing of any use to us. And there was an old tin teapot with one hundred and seventeen pounds in notes in it. I gather that Isabel Varran had been living on public assistance. She saved the money out of that, perhaps. There's no sign of investments or post office books...'

He paused and addressed Littlejohn.

'Do you want to take a look around, sir?'

There seemed little purpose in it if the local police had already done it. The whole place must have been barren and sad at the best of times. Now it was a pathetic relic of days gone by on its last legs. Even the scanty stock of clothing in the simple wooden chest in one corner of the room was mostly outmoded odds and ends of a past age.

Some long, voluminous dresses, a faded frock-coat... As though someone had collected the wardrobe for the traditional performance of *The Manx Wedding*, almost a genial mummers' tale, at which everybody dressed in early Victorian clothes. Finally, there appeared in a corner of the box a dilapidated bowler hat.

'Someone must have given them this old-fashioned finery,' commented Knell, carefully folding it back in the chest. 'Or else they bought it cheap at a rummage sale. This hat's had its day, too. Everybody had one of these hats for funerals in the old times. They'd have as soon gone naked as without a hat at a funeral. There was a sort of ceremonial about when you wore it and when you took it off. And if they kept bees, a bowler hat was always useful for draping a net over when they opened the hives...'

'When you've finished your little lecture on the social history of the Island, shall we get on with the murder case, Reginald? If Littlejohn doesn't think it necessary to go over the house again, shall we arrange our next move?'

'We ought to go to Close-e-Cass next and see Isabel Varran and the Candells. They'll probably have recovered from the first shock and be a bit more lucid than I found them when I first interviewed them.'

Littlejohn had been strolling here and there in the room, examining with interest the domestic odds and ends scattered around.

At right angles to the inside of the door had been constructed a rough wooden partition, a form of indoor porch, to keep out the draughts. On the back of this, inside the room, a couple of shelves had been rudely nailed up. These held one or two books, a number of medicine bottles and an old-fashioned sewing box.

Littlejohn opened the box, which was beautifully made, and lined in padded silk. It had evidently been treasured by a succession of owners. It contained nothing but a few bobbins of cotton, reels of silk, odds and ends of coloured material, needles, thimbles and scissors.

The books were old and bound in mouldy, crumbling leather. Littlejohn turned them over and looked through the pages. The Archdeacon, standing beside him, was interested.

'That is a Bible in Manx. Of very little practical use to the present generation, I'm afraid, but very valuable to a collector.'

He turned to the fly-leaf. It contained the names and dates of birth of past Varrans, written in various illiterate hands, yellow with age. Beside several of the names, a cross and a date, presumably of death.

'This is interesting, Tom...'

On one of the blank leaves a map had been roughly drawn.

'...You recollect how, in the legends of the old West in America, every prospector had an obsession that a rich lode of gold would be found in the vicinity of a chosen spot, and spent his life grubbing and fighting over it. The same applied, and, I suppose, still does, in certain places in these curraghs. It was believed, probably with some reason, that during the raids from the Norsemen in early times, treasure was hidden in the marshes, then known as the Myers, by natives and by the monks of an abbey which had a small foundation here. There is a plaintive Manx ballad about Mylecharaine, a miser, who found one of the hoards. It included the famous Mylecharaine silver cross, a lovely ornament which eventually disappeared, but not before details of it had been preserved and there is a replica of it now in the Manx museum. This map is perhaps one of many scattered among old curragh families, who hoped, one day, to make themselves rich by digging in the bogs and unearthing silver and gold. Let's see if we can identify it.'

The Archdeacon, who seemed to have forgotten the murder and his impatience to be getting on with the investigation, took the book and laid it on the table, put on his spectacles and bent over it.

'It is apparently a map of this locality. The rough oblong at the head of the map is obviously a small lough. It is marked *Polly*, probably the way an illiterate would spell *Poyll*, Manx for Pool. There were several such small lakes indicated on old maps; none exist now since the curraghs were drained.'

He looked closely over the top of his spectacles.

'You see the road is marked *Bayr Dhoo*, the Black Path. And here is Close Dhoo, this house. The land marked *Lheaney Streeu*, was surely of some importance for the name means Field of Strife. The site of a fight or a battle, either physically or by litigation. The Field of Strife was obviously not worth much for cultivating purposes, for here beside the name of it is the word *Creelagh* or Shaking Land, which means Bog. The strife may have arisen for right of turbary, or peat digging.

He straightened himself, closed and put the Bible away.

'This looks like another those treasure maps, of which dozens must have been in circulation at one time or another. Almost every family in the curraghs must have some map or legend which they hope will one day make them wealthy... But this is wasting time and has nothing to do with our murder. Shall we go and see the Candells?'

'Yes, sir. Would the Chief Superintendent like to see upstairs before we leave? It's a loft which Isabel Varran uses as a bedroom.'

'You've gone over it thoroughly, I presume, Knell?'

'Yes. There's nothing up there to excite anybody. A bed, another chest full of old clothes, no letters or papers, except some old shoe boxes filled with out-of-date Christmas cards and old family photographs. Nothing at all worth wasting any more time on.'

Knowing Knell's thoroughness, Littlejohn was sure what he said was right. In any event, a call at Close-e-Cass was the more important for the present and they could return later and give Close Dhoo a closer look-over. They locked up the house again and made their way.

Knell had to drive a considerable way back down the rutted lane along which they had come there, until they struck a properly metalled road. Otherwise the tyres and springs of the police car would have suffered from the flints and potholes of the road to Close-e-Cass which Isabel Varran and the Candells had used on the night before.

The weather had suddenly changed and grown cloudy and damp and as the trees on the roadside thinned around the cultivated fields, the landscape grew monotonous under the grey sky.

By a mild, unhurried farm road, or 'street', as they call them there, they soon reached Close-e-Cass, its buildings clean and white-washed surrounding the house like fortifications. The farmyard, with a huge dump of manure surrounded by a trench of brown drainage in one corner, was obviously a centre of activity and there was a small knot of men there all talking at once. The four Candell men, Joseph the father, Tom his brother, and the two sons, Joe and Baz, were prominent among them. Tom was a harmless family oddity who talked to himself a lot and emphasised his points by gesticulations and often roared with laughter at what he told himself. The morning milking had been finished and the full churns dispatched and in spite of the ragings of Joseph, the other three had resisted all his efforts to drive them to work in the fields. The compulsive curiosity of all peasants held them and they imagined they might be wanted by the police or some other vague authority and they hung about expectantly.

A thick, squat man of between fifty and sixty, Sydney Handy, the brother-in-law of Joss Varran, an officious farmer from Narradale, with a broad expressionless face and a tight seam of a mouth, was laying down the law about something and as he spoke he made little pecking jerks with his predatory nose like the beak of a buzzard. Although he never saw Isabel Varran or the dead man from one year to the next, he now felt himself of some importance in the case. He had a black eye and was walking with a limp, features which gave rise to plenty of humorous enquiries, which seemed to annoy him. He said he'd trodden on a hay-rake and the shaft had leapt up and hit him.

Wandering here and there, with a camera hanging round his neck, a lank newspaper man with pale, myopic eyes. He made straight for Knell with a curious sidling walk.

'Any developments, Reg?'

'You still here, Quick? Nothing more to report.'

'Is that the Scotland Yard detective who's a friend of yours...?'

There was no time for a reply. Mrs. Candell, who might have been waiting in ambush for Knell and his party to arrive, emerged from the house, crossed the yard and made straight for the Archdeacon, ignoring anyone else there. A strong, dumpy, full-bosomed woman who seemed to be seething with indignation at the disturbance of the usual morning peace of the place.

'I want a word with you, reverend, if you don't mind, indoors, out of the way of these busybodies … '

And she turned and began to return to the house as though there was no question of a refusal.

'Wait a moment, Mrs. Candell … '

She halted in her course, looking back over her shoulder.

'I shan't speak to anybody else but you and in private.'

She continued on her way without more ado.

'Do you mind, Tom?'

Littlejohn smiled and shook his head.

The Archdeacon followed the woman.

Littlejohn lit his pipe and looked around the place.

Nobody seemed to be taking much notice of the police. The aggressive brother-in-law was holding the field and arguing fiercely with the rest of the men of the family. Now and then he swept his arm in the direction of a tall tower constructed at one end of the house, one storey higher than the main building. It was plastered and white-washed in keeping with the rest of the place and a large tall window overlooked the farmyard. At this window an incongruous pair, an old man and a young woman, one sitting and the other standing, were watching all that was going on. Her hand was on the old man's shoulder. This scene seemed to be agitating the brother-in-law, Sydney Handy.

The old man, when he retired, had had this watch-tower constructed and moved in there. Thence he could watch all that went on in the farm and neighbourhood and he slept and ate there. Admission was forbidden without his consent and he had emphasised this by having a notice placed on the door of the ground floor which gave access to it. *Trespassers forbidden,* with all the s's reversed.

Junius Candell had started life as a sailor and then spent a spell as a fisherman before turning to farming with the money he had saved in his travels, for he was an avaricious man. In his young days he had visited strange faraway lands and, in cold weather, when he grew light-headed and delirious and took to his bed, he often thought himself in the antipodes, or in Kinsale, where the Manx herring fleet had once frequently put-in, and he called out the names of shipmates and girls who had taken his fancy during his wanderings.

Mr. Handy had arrived, full of his own importance, to represent the Varran family and to ask why Isabel had taken up quarters with the Candells instead of with her own sister at Narradale. Sydney was a great talker and had once been a local preacher. Words usually rolled out of him non-stop. But now he felt restricted and inhibited by the pair watching him from the tower window, like a couple of immortals in their heaven. Now and then, the girl made a remark to her companion and they both laughed.

'What are those two doin' spyin' on all that goes on? And I find nothing for them to be ribald about. This is a murder, I'll have you know, not a pantomime...'

The girl was of unusual beauty and it might have been that which was upsetting Mr. Handy, whose philandering in the course of his milk round was talked about and exaggerated and embroidered by the local gossips. Beulah Candell had dark hair framing an oval face and peculiar oriental slant eyes. She had a good ripe figure to match her good looks, too, and there was a strange magnetism about her which attracted men like bees to a honey-pot. She was watching Knell, the youngest of the men there outside her own family.

'That's old Junius Candell and his grand-daughter up there. Her name's Beulah.'

Knell said it following Littlejohn's gaze and lowering his own eyes nervously as he caught the bold glance of the girl above.

'Beulah's the apple of the old man's eye, they say. He won't let her work on the farm, so she just plays the lady.'

He didn't get any farther, as Joseph Candell, seeking an excuse for getting away from Mr. Handy, pretended with exaggerated gestures that he'd only just noticed the police and hurried to them.

'Any more news?' he said.

'How could there be?'

Knell said it impatiently. It was strange that, in the course of a crime investigation, people thought the case developed like a growing cabbage or a disease running its certain course, or a birth after gestation. A sort of scientific development, instead of a hotch-potch of information being painfully sorted out and sometimes a stroke of luck which led to a solution.

'I hear you've got some help from London ... '

Candell looked hard at Littlejohn. Knell introduced them.

'I was the first to find Joss Varran. That is, after his sister found him, or says she did ... '

And Candell put the same question to Littlejohn that he'd put to everyone he'd spoken to since the crime.

' ... If he was dead when she saw him there in the ditch, how did he get in the house? That's where I found him dead.'

'I was the first to find him.'

He said it again, as though there were some merit in it or a reward waiting somewhere for him.

'Did you know Joss Varran well, Mr. Candell?'

'I hardly knew him at all. The less I had to do with him, the better. A contentious man and violent when the drink was in him.'

Candell seemed flustered and kept blinking his red-rimmed eyes as though nervous about what was coming next.

'When did you last see him alive?'

'I must have been one of the last to see him before he shipped off on the trip that ended in him being sent to gaol.'

'Where did you see him?'

'In Ramsey. At the time he was working as a deck hand on the container ship that comes in from Preston. She was just leaving the quay and he was leaning over the rail.'

'Do you remember the date?'

Candell looked indignant.

'It was more than twelve months ago. I can't remember so far back.'

'Think again. You might recollect it...'

'I think it was a Friday. I was taking a stroll along the quay waiting for the wife, who I take to do her shopping in Ramsey every Friday.'

'So, it was a Friday then?'

'That's right. Yes; and it was, March, too, because I remember I'd run out of hay and our own wasn't ready. I bought some and I remember I'd just got my milk cheque and was going to pay it in at the bank along with some cash, and I used the cash to pay the merchant for the hay instead. The milk cheque comes in the last week in the month. It must have been the last week in March last year when I saw Joss Varran.'

All very tortuous, but useful.

'Did he say anything to you?'

'He shouted at me, otherwise I wouldn't have noticed him. He'd been drinking even then and was a bit cheeky.'

'What exactly did he say?'

Candell hesitated and looked sheepish.

'He shouted "What ho, Alfonso!" I ignored him.'

'Alfonso?' asked Knell. 'I've got you down here as Joseph.'

Candell kicked the paving-stones of the yard nervously.

'It's a nickname I had when I was younger. Varran had a cheek to use it. As though I was a pal of his.'

Joseph Candell had, in his youth, although to look at him now you wouldn't think it, been somewhat of a masher. Names like *Alfonso* and *The Count* were endowed on such fancy men by their contemporaries.

'And that was the last you saw of Joss Varran?'

'Till I found him dead at Close Dhoo.'

'You've no idea, then, who might have killed him?'

Joseph Candell felt he'd said quite enough already. In Celtic fashion, his mind ran well ahead of current events and he saw himself lost in the ramifications of a case in which he might become involved, ruined, disgraced, destroyed. Besides, his father from his lofty perch in the tower was making gestures which suggested that old Junius thought he'd done quite enough talking and that he and his family had better get on with their farming. Alfonso sheered off.

'I don't know anything else. I've told you all I know.'

'Alfonso, you don't happen to have a bottle of beer handy...?'

Candell leapt as though he'd been stung.

'What the hell!'

And he stopped. Alcohol and foul language were strictly forbidden at Close-e-Cass by Junius Candell, who'd once owned a private chapel of his own in the curraghs and preached in it, too, until the small congregation got tired of Junius behaving as though he were God himself and stopped attending.

'What are you doing here, you old loafer, and what do you want?'

He spoke to a small, wizened man with little cunning eyes glinting behind beetling grey brows, who had gradually sidled up to the group and had been listening quietly to all that was being said. He reminded Littlejohn of one of those Irish characters created by Barry Fitzgerald, of happy memory.

E. D. Cojeen was the local rag-and-bone man who, in exchange for the cast-offs of the neighbourhood, old clothes and anything else from a rare coin to a mowing machine or a mangle, gave coloured balloons, packets of detergent and tinned goods. Naturally, his wardrobe was extensive and almost every day he wore a different set of clothes, the best he had collected the day before. Now, he was togged up in a strange black coat with clawhammer tails and on his feet were a pair of splendid football boots.

'I seem to have asked for the wrong thing. I forgot that in this place wine is a mocker and strong drink is raging. I only wanted a drink for Bessie.'

And he indicated a little donkey, hitched to an empty cart, for, in his haste to reach the scene of the crime and obtain information to scatter in the course of his rounds, he had hitherto done no business. In his wanderings, E. D. Cojeen stopped at every pub and Bessie was as big a soak as he was himself.

'What do you want? You know very well we don't take kindly to the likes of you hanging around here.'

'I want to see the police. To be precise, Inspector Knell. It's about poor Joss Varran, of whom, we must now speak in the past tense. He *was*, and now *is not*.'

In the course of his wanderings and gatherings, E. D. Cojeen accumulated a lot of old books. These he read feverishly in his spare time. He often read them aloud to Bessie, who shared his home in a disued R.A.F. hut near Kirk Andreas. He boasted a good literary knowledge and style of speech, although nobody else agreed, for it was a sort of Irish stew of words and phrases he'd accumulated and which he trimmed and gabbled to suit the occasion.

'I have some information for the police. If I don't impart it, they will find out I have it and let the sun go down upon their wrath. Only a fool tries to outsmart smart people.'

Knell, who had met Cojeen before, was impatient.

'Tell us what it is without any embroidery, then. First, give me your name.'

'I intend to do that. I see the patriarch watching us from his tower in company with his chatelaine living there a life of queenly luxury. Before he descends and pursues Bessie and me with his avenging rod, I will tell you that I think I was the last man to see Joss Varran alive. You want my full name? Emanuel Dalrymple Cojeen.'

And he leaned back on the studs of his football boots and looked from one to another of them to observe the impact. Knell was astonished as he wrote it in his book. This was a revelation! The little man was generally known as Cojeen the Rags, and nobody ever bothered about his E. D.

'Well, goon.'

It was like opening a sluice-gate and releasing E. D. Cojeen's Irish stew of verbiage. Knell did his best to pick out the meat from the rest and put it in his book. It could hardly be described as an interview. It was a monologue. Knell couldn't get a question in edgeways.

It seemed that Cojeen and Bessie, after a good day's exchanges, had stopped several times for drinks at their favourite inns. In the last of their round, on the quay at Ramsey, they had found Joss Varran, standing at one end of the counter, sullenly drinking. He didn't recognise Cojeen and E. D., knowing him to be an awkward man in his cups, avoided him. As the bar clock struck nine, Varran drank up and left in a hurry.

Cojeen wondered how Joss was going to get home at that hour. There were no buses running and few people about to give him a lift. The rag-and-bone man hitched up Bessie in the inn yard and they started along the quay for home. Their cart was empty, as Cojeen rented a shabby little ware-house in Ramsey where he stored and sorted out his rum-mage. As soon as they reached the country road to Andreas, he would hoist himself on the cart and Bessie would tow him leisurely to their lodging and there, if he was asleep, which was usually the case, vigorously shake the shafts to remind him that she was hungry.

As they approached the swing-bridge, Cojeen made out Varran, leaning against the first stanchion. Cojeen hurried the donkey past, in case Joss stopped him and asked for a lift, which, in Mr. Cojeen's own words was a plausible and unconvincing impossibility. However, man and beast had only moved a few yards beyond him when a car arrived, picked up Joss and moved off noisily and at high speed.

'Did you see the car plainly or who was driving it?'

'I saw the silhouette of a man and also that of the car. I didn't recognise either and that is the truth.'

'And that is all?'

'Except a deduction, which as you know, might be proved fallacious. In the course of my profession, I have had some experience with cars, old cars principally. This was of very ancient vintage, but still in excellent running order. The acceleration ... the clarity of the ignition ... '

They were in the stew again.

'Briefly, what was the deduction?'

'An old Bentley, my friend, and in excellent condition. Old friends are best, aren't they? I must go. The patriarch is waving his stick at me.'

Chapter IV
Family Secrets

After the pandemonium going on in the farmyard, the interior of Close-e-Cass was quiet and peaceful. The Archdeacon was not surprised when Mrs. Candell pursued an independent line and removed herself from the public confusion created by the murder. He knew she came of better stock than her husband and he had, among many others, been surprised when she married into the Candell family at the very time when Junius was engaged in a furious quarrel with the Milk Board and had barricaded himself in his farm against its representatives and even fired shots at them. Whether she had found the blandishments of 'Alfonso' too much for her and had yielded to them, or whether she married him to rid herself of the grip of her own tyrannical father nobody seemed to know.

Mrs. Candell took the Archdeacon in the drawing-room and closed the door. It was a dark place, never used except when there was company, obscured by old trees blown at an angle by the prevailing high winds of winter. There was a smell of damp and mould about it. But it held the best furniture, including a set of Chippendale dining-chairs around a matching table, which Myra Candell had inherited from her own family and which she tended and polished herself in a sort of proud memorial ritual. There was a large mahogany dresser on one side, with a stuffed owl in the middle of it.

'Will you have a cup of tea, Archdeacon, or a glass of my ginger wine?'

'Ginger wine, if you please, Myra…'

He called her by her Christian name because he'd known her family well in the past.

'…I didn't know such sinful beverages were allowed in this house.'

'Grandfather thinks it's non-alcoholic. I see no reason for letting him know that it isn't. What a man doesn't know, he doesn't grieve over. I give him some for his chest in the cold weather and he doesn't suspect a thing and asks for more. It all goes to show that these rabid teetotallers don't know what they're talking about.'

She took two ruby glasses and a bottle from the sideboard and poured out a drink apiece.

'I'd better say what I have to say quickly, Mr. Kinrade, or else there'll be questions asked. It's about this murder of Joss Varran. You know Joss was a rascal, especially where women were concerned. And for some reason, women were attracted to him. Not always those of his own kind either. Some quite decent ones have found him fascinating.'

'I heard something of the kind…'

'Oh, I know when he was dressed in his working clothes and unwashed or drunk, he was a sorry, unattractive sight, but get him in his Sunday best, washed and shaved, at a show or a fair, you'd have looked twice at him. There was the Irish in him and he had dark good looks and the blarney. He seemed to appeal to younger women, too…'

The Archdeacon emptied his glass and put it on the table.

'Do I take it, Myra, that this fascination and good looks you're speaking of has somehow got Joss Varran in trouble with your own family?'

'How did you know that?'

'This tête-à-tête which you've engineered with me instead of with the police, Myra, must concern some confidential information and, as you seem to be excusing your own sex by enumerating Joss's powers over them, it might be that you were leading to a confession of importance in this murder business. I've always known you as a steady woman and unlikely to go off the rails yourself. Can it be that Beulah is involved?'

Without any warning Myra Candell burst into tears.

'I'm at my wits' end. I must tell somebody and you were the only one I could confide in. When I saw you arrive, I knew what I must do. I hope it isn't so, but I'm afraid that one of my family might be concerned with this crime.'

'Take another glass of your own ginger wine, Myra, and then calm down and tell me all about it. My friend Chief Superintendent Littlejohn, from London, is staying with me. He will surely be of help if you need him.'

She forgot her tears in her indignation.

'If you're going to go to the police with what I tell you, I might as well go to them myself and save you the trouble. What I had to say was for your ears alone and I wanted your advice, not for you to go to the police.'

'Tell me what's troubling you and I will advise you what to do. It shall all be in confidence unless you tell me I may pass it on to the proper quarter.'

'You are a good man and I trust you. I've been worried out of my wits since the murder of Joss Varran and I must trust somebody to help me. It's this. Our Baz...his name's Basil, but we call him that for short...our Baz hated Joss

Varran. Baz is usually a quiet, good-natured, inoffensive lad and I've never known him hate anybody in his life before.'

The parson could believe it. He had known Baz from childhood. A good-tempered giant, always smiling, always ready to do anybody a good turn. Perhaps not very well endowed with brains and general intelligence, but a well-mannered, gentle type and a steady worker.

'How old is Baz? In his middle thirties?'

'Thirty-two. He's the eldest. He had a quarrel with Joss and they had a fight. It was Baz who started it. He admitted that, and knowing him and his strength, you'd have thought he'd have killed Joss Varran. Instead, Joss half-killed our Baz. Joss had been in the commandos in the war and it seems he'd learned that sort of fighting you see on the television. He gave Baz an awful beating; he even kicked him in the face. Baz was in a terrible mess…'

She wrung her hands at the thought of it.

'Our Joe wanted to go with Baz and the two of them thrash Varran together, but Baz wouldn't. He said he'd deal with Joss in his own good time. None of us would have known what it was all about. Baz said he'd been kicked by one of the cows. We knew it wasn't true. It would have taken a mad horse to make him like he was; all bruised and bleeding and knocked about. I don't know how he managed to crawl home in the condition he was in. No; it was Joss Varran who told everybody what happened. He got drunk and started boasting in a public house.'

'And Baz has nursed his grievance ever since. When did this happen?'

'Not long before Joss left on the trip when he got arrested. Don't you see? It might look as though Baz was waiting and took the first opportunity.'

'Did he ever mention Varran again?'

'Not a word. He's not been the same man since that night. And now that Varran has been killed, suspicion is sure to fall on our Baz, because everybody in the neighbourhood knows about the bad blood between them. The police are certain to hear of it and question him, or even arrest him if he doesn't answer properly the questions they ask him.'

'Why shouldn't he answer questions properly?'

She hesitated.

'To tell you the truth, he never was very clever with his brains. He's a good worker with his hands. None better. But he's not a good talker. Gets his ideas mixed up if there's any complications being discussed. The police could easily trap him if they talked a lot to him...'

'No, Myra. They won't do that. If they ask him any questions at all, they'll give him a fair chance to answer them. They'll even help him with them, knowing him to be a decent, well-meaning man.'

'I hope so. I can say this, too. Baz was nowhere near Close Dhoo when all that was going on. He was here with us, looking in at the telly till about ten and then he went to bed. Joe and Baz sleep in the same room. Baz has only the family to support him. What do you call it...?'

'Give him an alibi.'

'That's it. And I'm frightened the police will think we've all arranged together to shield him. But I swear...He's a truthful man is our Baz.'

'Don't worry, Myra. If Baz tells the truth, they'll believe him. What was the quarrel about?'

Her mouth tightened.

'I don't want that bringing in the matter. It doesn't concern the police.'

'But it does...'

And the Archdeacon recollected Myra Candell's bitter words about Joss Varran as a woman chaser, a sort of country Don Juan, and he remembered, too, the daughter of the Candell house, the girl whose breathtaking beauty was the talk of the locality and made men want to fight for her. She always dressed in her finery as though she was going to a garden-party or a hunt ball, but she possessed a lot less in the way of good sense and wits than her elder brother, Baz, whose defects were tempered by his innocence.

'But it does. Was it something concerning Beulah?'

Mrs. Candell was undecided whether or not to end the conversation or continue it and disclose the truth.

'I wouldn't have told anybody else this, because, although I'm sure there's been gossip about it, nobody but the family knew what really happened. I told you Joss Varran had a bad reputation where women were concerned. Well, it seems he took a fancy to our Beulah. They met at the Ramsey Show and after that he was seen hanging about here and wherever she went. As I said, when he was dressed up to please, Joss Varran was a good-looking man and Beulah seems to have found him so. They got to meeting secretly. Beulah used to go visiting friends in the vicinity and I found out that often when she said she was going to a certain one of them, she never went there at all.'

'She was meeting Varran?'

'Yes. But I didn't find it out myself. They kept it very dark. She told me after he'd jilted her. I was terribly upset. You see, she's not a woman of the world and wouldn't be up to the tricks of a man like Joss Varran, who had no principles at all. She's developed into a good-looking girl, although I say it myself, but she was weakly as a child and spent a lot of time at home and her schooling was neglected. Also, with her being the only girl in the family of her generation, her grandfather has spoiled her. Nothing is too much for her where he's concerned. You understand?'

The Archdeacon understood perfectly what her mother was trying to express in a roundabout way. Beulah Candell was locally known as somewhat of a simpleton in spite of her looks.

'How old is Beulah?'

'Twenty-four.'

'And, just when did this affair with Joss Varran occur?'

'The year before he was sent to prison. Thank God it didn't go any further. It was obvious that Varran tired of her; she wasn't his sort. But she took it badly. Wouldn't eat and kept weeping for no apparent reason. She wouldn't tell any of us what had happened or why she took on so. It was her grandfather who got it out of her in the end. He and Beulah have always been fond of one another and he has a way with him in weedling things out of her. Sheds tears and says he won't be with us long and he's a poor old man who nobody wants or cares for. I suppose he kept on and on at her. In the end she told him. He nearly went off his head. I'm sure if he'd been younger and could get about, he'd have killed Joss Varran himself. As it was, he kicked up an awful family row and went for me and my husband for not taking proper care of Beulah. It seemed to act like a tonic to Beulah, having the whole family in an uproar about her. She was soon herself again.'

'And what about Baz?'

'Baz and Beulah have always been close, too. They're a bit alike. Never did much at school, never very sociable with other people, because other people talked a lot about all sorts of things and Baz and Beulah couldn't keep up with them. They understood one another and our Baz looked after Beulah and was always on her side.'

'And he took this matter with Varran to heart?'

'He did; but the rest of us didn't know it. He understood what had been happening, but he never said a word. Never a threat or a reproach about Joss Varran, but he must have thought and brooded a lot and finally made up his mind what to do and have a showdown with Joss. I told you what happened. Baz came out very badly.'

'And you fear the police might get to know about it and think Baz murdered Joss Varran?'

'I don't know, but I wanted you to know what happened and perhaps you'll put in a good word for Baz if he is suspected. Tell the police he's a good man and how he was at home all that night when the crime was committed. In fact, he was in bed when Isabel Varran came here for help and he went with his father and our Joe to see what it was all about. There's no guile or craft in Baz's nature and I'm sure if he had done anything to Varran he'd have said so.'

'I'll remember what you have told me, Myra, Chief Superintendent Littlejohn is an old friend of mine and I can trust him implicitly. I'm sure you ought to agree to my telling him what you've just said to me. Don't take on about it. If Baz did commit the crime, and I'm sure he didn't, the truth will come out. It would be far better for the police to know beforehand what happened between the two men than to find it out later.'

She sighed and shook her head.

'You'd better tell him then, if that's your advice. It's stupid to ask for a wise man's advice and then not take it. Very well, then. Tell him and ask him what we'd better do.'

'That's better. I'll see that Baz comes to no harm through it.'

'As for who committed the crime, there are plenty of people hereabouts who'll be glad to know he's dead. Beulah

wasn't the first girl he'd let down. And this isn't the first family that's had trouble and commotions through his fancying
their girls.'

'Is that so? Did he desert Beulah for another girl?'

'From what I hear he'd been seen hanging about
Ballakee Manor before he left here for the last time.'

'That's almost at the back door of his own home, Close
Dhoo?'

'Yes. The Duffys live there. A retired colonel and his
niece, Sarah. Sarah's Joss Varran's sort without any doubt,
although she's far above his class. I guess with her kind it's
come-day go-day with the men. If a man takes her fancy,
nothing else matters.'

'I've never met the Duffys. Ballakee Manor was empty
when last I heard of it. Who are they?'

'They arrived from England and bought the place and
tidied it up about three years ago. As you know, it's a house
with a poor reputation, and it's damp and surrounded by
bog land. People have always been coming and going there;
one tenant after another. Some call him Colonel Duffy; others plain Mister. He doesn't mix much with people and I've
heard of him snubbing those who tried to be neighbourly.
They tell me he drinks heavily. I've only seen him at a distance, so I couldn't say for certain anything about him. She's
different. Rides about the countryside on a horse and drives
a fast car. She's talkative enough, especially with the men.
She frequents the public houses in the locality and there's
always some man or other hanging round her. I've never
seen her close to, either, but that's what I'm told. One has to
be careful what one says about people when one can't prove
it. It might land one in trouble for slander. So, I'll ask you
not to repeat what is just gossip, Archdeacon. It's also said
that she's not the Colonel's niece, but just a woman who's

living with him. If that's the case, he's good reason to be jealous of her...'

'And she and Joss Varran were intimate?'

'I won't go so far as to say that. Joss was seen hanging round the manor and as he was hardly likely to get much of a welcome from the Colonel, it must have been the woman he was after. Perhaps the Colonel got mad at him and grew jealous and killed him...'

'I haven't given it a thought, but it's obvious that the police will have to turn their attentions to Ballakee if Joss Varran had some connection with the Duffys. Why should they be interested in a layabout like Joss?'

'As I said, he could be quite presentable when he was spruced up and clean in his best clothes.'

'We'll have to investigate that. Is there anything else, Myra?'

'No, I don't think so just at present. If grandfather had been in his prime, it might have been him who was mixed up with Joss. He and Beulah are as thick as thieves and she's the apple of his eye. She tells him everything, too, and they spend a lot of time together. He was in such a rage about Joss and Beulah that I thought he'd have a stroke.'

'But he soon got over it apparently.'

'Beulah soon forgot it and he calmed down and they got on better than ever. He gives her anything she asks for. Buys her clothes and all sorts of presents. If she asked for the moon, he'd do his best to get it for her.'

Outside the party seemed to be breaking up. They had talked themselves out and the fat man, Joseph Candell, had flown in a violent rage and driven his family to work. Syd Handy, too, was receiving short shrift and departed gesticulating and protesting to get on with his belated delivery of milk and to receive the abuse of his customers as well for his tardy appearance. In the distance E. D. Cojeen and his donkey were visible trundling along one of the dilapidated curragh roads. He was talking to her as was his custom and they seemed the happiest pair alive on that lamentable morning.

Knell had gathered very little useful information. The brothers Joe and Baz could add nothing to the account their father had given about the night of the crime. The family, it seemed, had assembled for the evening meal after the finish of the day's work and none of them had stirred from the house for the rest of the night. All of them, except old Junius and Beulah, had watched television until they had either fallen asleep in their chairs or retired pop-eyed to bed. The old man and his granddaughter had spent their time perusing a large mail order catalogue which had come by post earlier in the day and in the course of a detailed scrutiny and critical assessment, had decided what would suit Beulah to wear and old Junius to buy for her.

Littlejohn smoked his pipe and enjoyed the general atmosphere of the farmyard which seemed to have assumed the features of a small market day, farmers and their hangers on talking craftily about their affairs, but now mainly about the crime and its results. This was Littlejohn's first experience of the peculiar nature of curragh farming. The surrounding silence which made the voices of the talkative ones sound louder. The flat fields, broken here and there by placid little gleaming pools and stretches of bogland. The low, thick-growing bushes which divided the fields. The lush growths of bog myrtle, gorse, willow and hawthorn. The sturdy, healthy cattle which, after the draining of the marshes, had taken the place of the poor stock which waded for food among the sloppy meadows.

Joseph Candell, having at last disposed of most of his visitors, looked around for his wife and found her missing.

'What's happened to my missus?' he asked Knell aggressively, as though the Inspector had carried her off as a principal suspect.

'She went indoors with the Archdeacon...'

Although he was a man of small imagination, Joseph Candell was jealous of any relations his wife ever had with the opposite sex, whatever his age or condition. This was a mental kink dating from the day when he first saw his daughter with the slanting eyes... He need not have worried. He did not know, although his father did and kept it secret, that far back in their family tree, one of his ancestors, Captain Vitus Candell, master of the *Ramsey Town,* had returned to the Isle of Man with a Chinese bride. She had been regarded as a heathen in those days and least said, soonest mended...

Joseph Candell's shouts echoed round the farmyard.

'Myra! Myra!'

She appeared at once, followed by the parson and met her husband at the door. He eyed the pair of them suspiciously.

'Where have you been? I've been looking everywhere...'

'Minding my own business.'

Her husband was taken aback by this unusual curtness. She knew all about his philanderings in the days when he was 'Alfonso', but had never once flung them in his teeth.

'You've been getting on with the dinner, I hope. Although I must say where work is concerned, nobody's earned any dinner today. They've wasted hours talking... Where's Isabel Varran? Inspector Knell wants to see her.'

Hitherto, Knell had been unable to elude the crowd of chattering, quarrelling men who had seemed to fill the farmyard and overwhelmed him with their useless information and theories about the murder. They had even involved him in their arguments about the funeral and where it should take place, and Mr. Handy, through marriage the nearest relative of the victim, had even threatened to go to see the bishop about it all. Nobody except Knell had given Isabel Varran a thought. That was the way everybody treated Isabel. She was a cipher, a woman everybody walked past without even noticing.

'She's gone back to Close Dhoo. I couldn't stop her. She said she'd things to attend to.'

Knell intervened.

'When did she go, Mrs. Candell? I've got the key.'

'Just before you got here. There's a spare key hidden in the shed.'

'We'd better be off then and find out what this is all about. I've some questions I want to ask her.'

'You can stay to dinner if you like. It's nearly time.'

Joseph Candell seemed greatly relieved when they declined with thanks. He wasn't as hospitable as his wife. In fact, he wasn't hospitable at all. Feeding his hungry, aged father, his useless daughter and his brother who was a bit weak in his wits was, he felt, quite enough without expanding his table to outsiders.

'Sorry, Myra. But Inspector Knell is a busy man and has a lot to do before lunch. We'd better go, thank you.'

At this, Beulah and the old man appeared from the tower. She was wearing a flowered frock of low cut which, in his preaching days, her grandfather would have consigned to hell and her with it. Now, whatever she did was all right to him. He was wearing a quaint looking dressing-gown, which seemed to have been made from a large carriage-rug with a hole cut in it for him to put his head through. He was sucking chlorodine lozenges with a peculiar sideways thrust of the jaws. The strong blast of the cough drops, the exotic scent of Beulah and the aroma of the manure heap in the corner of the farmyard seemed to struggle for mastery.

Junius Candell was very old, but he dominated the scene with his wild white hair and his cold, stony, opaque eyes. He seemed to see only the Archdeacon and fixed him with an unblinking stare.

'Good day to you, Caesar. You keep strange company these times. But then, you always did.'

'Good day to you, too. I've just brought a great friend of mine, Chief Superintendent Littlejohn, to introduce him to the curraghs...'

'Is he the London man I hear about?'

He gave Littlejohn a curt nod.

Beulah was anxious not to be neglected. She shook hands all round with the visitors and gave Knell a sideways glance with those queer slant eyes of hers which made him blush.

'You know Inspector Knell of our own police, don't you, Junius?'

'I've heard of him. I knew his father, John Sebastian Knell. I prefer to deal with older, senior men, not young cubs. I came down to give the Chief Superintendent a bit of information that he might otherwise overlook. It's just this. Not only was there a murder the other night. Somebody was digging in the Shaking Field, as well. They tried to hide it afterwards by smoothing it over, but from up there...'

He pointed to the top of his tower with his stick.

'... Up there, there's not much that we miss, is there, Beulah, girl?'

And they both laughed, the girl with a giggle and the old man with a noise like a quacking duck.

'It's the nearest place to heaven up there. We see all that goes on.'

Beulah thought something was expected of her. She addressed Knell fiercely.

'It served Joss Varran right. He had it coming to him.'

The adoring old man gave her a satisfied smile at the thought that she was happy about it all.

CHAPTER V
THE SECRET OF THE BOG

There was a hotel in Ballaugh and Knell said he knew the proprietor. He would give them some sandwiches and beer and there they could talk over the confusion of the morning's labours and discuss their next move.

The sky had cleared and now the sun was struggling through. The air was extraordinarily limpid for the time of year. They passed a church with a tower like a wedding cake and drove across a level crossing of the now disused railway. After the depression of Close-e-Cass, Littlejohn felt his spirits rise. It was like another world.

A small, clean village built around crossroads: one from the curraghs, one to Ramsey, another to Peel, and the fourth vanished into a leafy glen and then up into the hills. There were groups of white-washed cottages here and there and a handsome Georgian house or two. The prowling speculative builders didn't seem to have, as yet, arrived to despoil the place.

They found the hotel and the landlord, who was having a glass of beer with two customers, one in a tweed hat and the other in a white cap, came to welcome them. There was an intimate atmosphere about the place and the owner seemed anxious to please. He shook hands with Knell, who introduced him to his companions. The landlord said his father had often spoken about the Archdeacon appreciatively, and he was not at all intimidated by Littlejohn.

'I've read about him in the Sunday papers. I can't say I'd much time for Joss Varran, but I hope you catch whoever murdered him. This is a peaceful island and we've no time for violence.'

'Can you find us some food, Charlie?'

'Sorry, we haven't anything hot. But there's some nice beef for sandwiches.'

'Just the thing. And some beer.'

'Right. I'll serve them in the little room; then, if you want to talk business, private like, you won't be disturbed.'

He took them to a small, cosy room off the main bar, on the way politely introducing them to his two customers, much to their satisfaction. They hurriedly drank-up and went into the village to tell everybody that Scotland Yard was on the job, they'd met the Chief Superintendent, and that whoever had committed the crime had better prepare for the worst.

The Archdeacon told Littlejohn and Knell of his interview with Myra Candell. It gave them more insight into the characters of Joss Varran and Beulah Candell, and revealed Baz's hatred of the dead man and the reason for it. It also gave Baz an alibi of sorts but there was little by way of a lead in it. Except that the Duffys of Ballakee Manor had now entered the picture. Joss Varran had taken a fancy to Sarah Duffy, it seemed, and had, before his imprisonment, been found hanging round Ballakee.

Most of the conversation over lunch was small talk about the crime, but led nowhere. The motley gathering at Close-e-Cass had precluded much in the way of those quiet interviews which are much more revealing than the shouted opinions of a crowd.

Isabel Varran had to be questioned and she had presumably gone home after her disappearance from Close-e-Cass. They decided that the Archdeacon was best equipped for dealing with a rather ticklish intrusion on her silence and reticence.

Meanwhile, Littlejohn and Knell would pay the inhabitants of Ballakee a visit and try to find out their relations with Joss Varran.

And the quaint statement of Junius Candell that someone had been digging in the Shaking Ground aroused Littlejohn's curiosity. The Archdeacon had quite a lot to say about it.

'The word *Creelagh,* in the old Manx language meant shaking or quaking ground, in other words, bogland. The map we saw at Close Dhoo in the Manx Bible, indicated a patch of it in the field adjacent to the house. This may have been a source of peat for the cottage fire, but this particular spot might have been more important than a peat digging to merit its record in the family Bible. Why this place should be indicated when there are plenty of others in the vicinity makes it seem more than a mere turbary, as these turf cuttings are called over here...'

'You mean there might be some hidden treasure there?'

'Hardly. The universal obsession with treasure in the bogs has probably resulted, in the course of years, in the whole place being turned over again and again in search of them and the Varrans would be among the rest in sifting their neighbouring land. But there's no doubt the natives here hid things in the peat. For example, kegs of butter were often sunk there to preserve them until their contents were needed. The turf is firm now that the bogs have been drained and anything sunk in it at a reasonable depth is sealed from the air by it and kept in good condition. You know, Reginald, the nature of bog oak, the trunks of old trees, not only prevented from rotting, but hardened and excellent for furniture. Relics of all kinds have been found in the peat. There was, too, the skeleton of a great deer preserved there in such good condition that it was reassembled with great skill by Thomas Kewish, the blacksmith of Ballaugh, and accepted by the museum in Edinburgh ... '

Knell was wondering what all this was about and what it had to do with the crime. He smiled benignly at the Archdeacon, however, to show that he wasn't bored.

'Junius Candell says the Shaking Field near Close Dhoo was disturbed during the night when Joss Varran returned. Did Joss do it? And what was he seeking? And was he killed on account of it?'

Littlejohn nodded.

'That's a good theory which may give us a break at last. The first thing to do is to find the spot which was disturbed and dig there, isn't it?'

'Yes, I think so. Except that probably what had been hidden in the peat was removed either by Joss or his murderer. We may find something useful, however. But I suggest that first I speak to Isabel Varran and try to find if she knows anything about this queer hiding-place. Its indication on the map in the Bible would surely make it a topic of family discussion. We can find out what it was used for and exactly where it's situated. We'll meet again, I suggest, and continue the search after you've had a talk with the occupants of Ballakee Manor and I have questioned Isabel.'

Their sandwiches finished, the landlord arrived with some tasty apple pie and cream, the former presumably fresh from the refrigerator judging from its temperature.

They ended their meal, thanked their host, and left him to make the most of their visit among the unusual number of customers arriving inquisitively for an unaccustomed afternoon glass of beer.

Knell drove the Archdeacon along the rough track to Close Dhoo and pulled up at the ramshackle garden gate. He and Littlejohn waited in the car whilst the Archdeacon made sure that there was someone at home. There was no sense in leaving the parson stranded there for maybe an hour if Isabel Varran was elsewhere.

In answer to Mr. Kinrade's knock, however, there was a gentle movement of the curtain on one side of the door, which was quickly opened when Isabel Varran saw who was there. She stood in silence until the Archdeacon spoke.

'Good afternoon, Isabel. You remember me don't you?'

She seemed quite placid now and to have got over much of the recent ordeal. She nodded her head.

'You're the Venerable Archdeacon, aren't you? I remember you at the church anniversary at Andreas. I even remember your preaching text...'

Her smile was almost arch.

'... It was "Occupy till I come".'

The Archdeacon was taken aback. That was at least fifteen years ago!

'Come in. I expect you've called about Joss's funeral.'

The Archdeacon gave Knell a wave of his hand to show that all was well and the Inspector waved back, reversed the car in a nearby field gateway and drove off.

Isabel Varran seemed to have been at her housework. There was a brush and a dust-pan on the floor and she whisked these away and dusted one of the chairs in front of the cold fire.

'Sit down, Mr. Kinrade.'

She was now dressed in black from head to foot; an old-fashioned black blouse and an out-of-date calf-length skirt. She was in no way distraught, but her manner was grave and dignified, which she evidently thought in keeping with the present situation.

'They'll bury Joss in the churchyard, won't they? He'll not have to be...'

The Archdeacon had no idea what she thought the alternative would be. He interrupted her to assure her that Joss would get a decent burial in the place she wished. She seemed relieved and relaxed and took a seat opposite him.

'Is there anything else I can do, Isabel?'

'No. My sister's husband, Sydney Handy, has taken charge of it all.'

That would be more than enough! Mr. Handy, for his own and the family's reputation, would attend to everything down to the last detail, including the funeral feast afterwards.

'You will not be staying here until after the funeral, at least?'

'Why not? It is my home. The Candells have been very good to me. We haven't been friendly with them for years and it was good of them to be so kind. But I can't take advantage of them any more. I'll be all right at home.'

'I'm very sorry about Joss and all the upset and shock you've had. Would you like to talk to me about him?'

'There isn't anything to say. He's been away for more than a year and before that he wasn't at home much.'

'He was at sea, wasn't he?'

'If you could call it that. Before he... before he was in prison, he was on a cargo boat that ran between Preston and Ramsey. They call it container traffic. I don't exactly know what that is, but he seemed to earn good money.

Sometimes, the boat went to London. It was on one of the London trips that he got himself in trouble.'

'How did you manage to live, Isabel? Did he send you money?'

'I did cleaning for a lady in Ballaugh.'

'But that's over two miles away. How did you get there?'

'I walked. It didn't seem far.'

He could imagine her doing it, in all kinds of weather, patiently, without complaint. There weren't many of her kind left now.

'And now...?'

'Mrs. Simister died eighteen months ago. She stamped a National Health card for me and now I've got a pension. I'm sixty-two, you know.'

She didn't look it. She had an ageless look about her, like a nun, whose years were hard to guess.

'And you didn't see much of Joss, even when he was working on the boats?'

'Sometimes he'd take a day or two off and once a year he took his holidays. Even then he didn't always stay here. He came and went.'

'Was he courting any of the local girls?'

She didn't seem in the least excited by the question.

'Not that I know. He never talked to me about anything like that and, as I didn't go out much, I never heard of it.'

'I didn't know Joss at all. He must have been one of the younger members of the family. What was he like?'

'He was the next to the youngest and I was the oldest. He was big and well made.'

She rose to her feet and went in the kitchen. He could hear her rummaging about and then she appeared with a postcard in her hand.

'He had this in his things. He must have had it taken somewhere on his travels. It isn't a bad likeness, as he was before he went to prison. He'd changed when he came back. I had to identify him. He'd gone thin and pale while he was away.'

The Archdeacon looked at the photograph. It had been taken in the street somewhere, probably by one of those peripatetic photographers who snap you suddenly and then take your money and give you their address from which they post their handiwork to you. It showed a tallish, well-built, smiling man, with dark eyes and features and a head of tousled curly hair. Mrs. Candell had mentioned Joss's good looks. The Archdeacon could imagine Joss attracting some of the opposite sex who liked them that way. He had an air about him of impudence and self-satisfaction.

Isabel seemed disturbed by the sight of the picture. She began to weep silently.

'Somebody killed him. Why him? It wasn't robbery. His money was in his pocket. And his watch. What could it have been for? It must have been somebody who ought to be in the asylum, somebody mad...'

She calmed down and sat opposite the Archdeacon again, wiping her eyes and blowing her nose.

'Did the police give you his things?'

'No. I asked them for the photograph. I didn't want it to get lost. It was of Joss as I knew him before he lost weight and his face got thin and they close clipped his hair...'

She paused as though ready for another burst of tears, but controlled herself.

'They didn't seem to believe me when I said I found Joss in the hedge opposite here. The Candells said he was in the house in a chair. Well, when the police saw the hedge and the ditch and how they was trampled about and found blood there, they knew what I said was true. What I can't understand, too, is that Joss's kit-bag with his things in it was missing. Whoever did it, must have taken it with him.'

She hadn't got over her annoyance at having her word doubted.

'Did Joss have any enemies?'

She gave the Archdeacon a fearful look, as though the word enemy had some menace for her, too.

'I don't know. The only part of his life that I know of is the few odd days he spent here between his journeys. Even then, he often slept on the boat. He mainly turned up here when he was short of money and borrowed from me, or if I didn't want to find him money, he took it.'

'How did he treat you when he came home?'

'Not like a sister, if that's what you mean. He ate and slept here and wanted money. Sometimes he came in drunk. It was surprising how he found his way here when he was drunk...But I ought not to be talking like this, him being dead. But everybody knows about him, although it wasn't me who told them. Syd Handy, my brother-in-law, once tried to get Joss to mend his ways and Joss got mad at him and chased Syd out of the house. All the neighbourhood got to hear about it. I suppose Syd talked a lot on his milk round...'

'Do you know the Duffys at Ballakee Manor, Isabel?'

'I know of them, that's all. Miss Duffy, or it might be Mrs. Duffy, I don't know which, rides past here on a horse sometimes. She rides all over the curraghs.'

'You've not met either of them?'

'No. Although, as the crow flies, you might say they're our nearest neighbours.'

'Did Joss know them?'

'Not that I'd know. As I told you, he never had much talk with me. I never knew who was his friends and who wasn't. If he knew them, he never mentioned it.'

'Your sister might know?'

'He wouldn't have anything to do with her. They never got on and whenever they met they had a row. But Syd Handy might know. There's not much goes on in these parts that Syd doesn't hear about.'

They might have been in a world apart. Between the questions and the answers there was a dead silence, except for the monotonous ticking of the alarm clock on the sideboard. Small wonder that Isabel Varran was reputed to be a queer one. Silence most of the time. Nobody to talk to but herself. Not even a cat or a dog. And this had gone on for years. In the course of her solitary confinement, she seemed to have forgotten certain words and had to pause to bring them back to mind. But she had not deteriorated in her solitude. There was a kind of self-reliance about her and a refinement manifest in the neatness of the house and her personal appearance. She was simple and straightforward in her replies to the Archdeacon's questions.

'Do you know a field called the Creelagh, Isabel?'

She seemed puzzled.

'The Shaking Field, then?'

'Oh, yes, I know that. Part of it goes with this house, but we never use it. It's peat-land. Whoever owned this house or was a tenant, had the right to cut peat from the Shaking Field. My father used to cut turf and we burned it. I don't use peat. My sister brings me wood in the van whenever I get short.'

'Has anyone been digging there recently?'

She gave him a surprised look as if he'd gone slightly off his head.

'Whatever would they dig there for? I've not been there for years, but nobody but the occupier of the house would be allowed to do anything in our part. It's in the deeds.'

'Didn't people used to store things like butter in small kegs or boxes there in the old days?'

'We never had butter enough to store it. We never had any cattle...'

She paused.

'I remember, though, when I was a girl...But perhaps I ought not to tell you. It was a secret and my father said he'd thrash us if we ever told anybody...'

'He's been dead for years. Couldn't you tell me what it was about as, I'm sure, no harm could come of it after all this time?'

She was silent again and then seemed to make up her mind.

'You're sure the police couldn't do anything about it if they got to know, because I believe father would have had to go to gaol if he'd been found out?'

The Archdeacon's imagination began to work. Could he have hidden a body there, or a treasure of some sort? Perhaps stolen goods or illegal weapons of some kind.

'You know my father came to the Isle of Man from Ireland. County Kerry. He had a recipe for making something with a lot of pipes and a boiler. He used to brew it in the kitchen and then he hid the pipes and the boiler and a small tub in the bog, because if the police found them it would be hard with him.'

'Was he making poteen?'

'I don't know what it was called, but he sometimes got drunk on it. He used potatoes. He had them in tubs in the kitchen.'

'Surely, he didn't tell you all this? How old were you then, Isabel?'

'About ten. He certainly didn't tell me. But there are few secrets between people living in a house like this. My sister and me slept in a bed in this room and the boys in the loft. My father and mother and two younger sisters slept in a bed in that corner. When they thought we were asleep, they used to talk. Mother didn't like him making his drink. He'd bring men in now and then and give them some and they'd start singing and shouting and my mother had to stop them coming, because someone would hear them and she was frightened the police would find out. My sister was too young to trouble at all, but I would be awake, pretending to be asleep and I heard all the arguing between my parents about it. I never saw my father actually making the stuff, because we were put to bed early when he was busy with it in the kitchen with the front door locked and a chair wedged behind it to make double sure.'

'And he hid the apparatus in the bog, in the Shaking Field?'

'Yes. I know, because my mother was afraid someone would find it there. She said she hoped it would sink and vanish in the bog, but he said the place where he hid it had peat as solid as boards and there was no fear of that. I remember it all as plain as if it was yesterday, because I was afraid of it all. You see, my father got drunk on his stuff and then, when my mother argued with him, he used to beat her ... '

She paused.

'Trouble. Always trouble for as long as I can remember. You think it's all over and you can have a bit of peace. And then, back it comes. Now it's Joss and he's got himself killed. First my father and mother quarrelling, then Joss disturbing the house when I'd got it all nice and quiet and cosy, and now he's been murdered and the police are about the place. I wonder what will be next.'

She seemed too sunk in despair even to weep.

71

The Archdeacon did his best to comfort her, promised the police would bother her as little as possible, and when it was all over, he'd do his best to see that she was settled back in quiet and comfort again.

She offered him tea and he, afraid to upset her by refusing and thinking the preparation might take her mind off her present distress, accepted. She produced some home-made soda cakes which were surprisingly good and he was able to tell her truthfully that the tea, probably made with soft spring water, was the nicest he'd tasted for many a day.

Chapter VI
Ballakee

Knell prided himself on his knowledge of the curragh roads and tracks, but the way to Ballakee Manor almost defeated him. They could see the house from the car, but he circumnavigated it two and a half times before he found the gravel approach which led to the entrance gates to the park, if such desolation merited the name. The gates were open and looked as if they'd never been shut for years; the hinges of one had rusted away and it had been fastened askew by a piece of rope to one of the shabby pilasters. The house was visible in the distance, set among an unkempt four or five acres of wild bramble and gorse. An attempt had been made at some time to introduce order there and there were traces of flower beds, a few decayed garden ornaments and a tumbledown summer house visible, but the present tenants had obviously left everything to go to ruin.

'It's not a manor house at all...'

Knell had told Littlejohn as much of the history of the place as he knew.

'...It was a smallish farm and was empty for a long time. Then a man called Egerton bought it and sold off all the land except that near to the house and spent a lot of money enlarging it and improving it. He must have been off his head spending so much on a place miles from anywhere in a spot like this. They say he'd been an official in the colonies. He had two Chinese servants and lived in seclusion. He got in trouble for setting his dogs on intruders. Then, one day, he and his staff left the house, just as it was with the furniture in it, and went away without a word. News came later that he'd gone over to England to see a doctor and had died there. The manor was emptied and tidied up and the Duffys took it over. It's said there's something wrong with the title to the place; the deeds have been lost, or something. However, Colonel Duffy seems to have settled in after a fashion. Judging from the ruin of the grounds he, too, might be a bird of passage.'

They drew up at the front door after running over a gravel path almost obliterated by moss and overgrown bushes.

The house, which was not without charm, had a forlorn, forgotten look in the middle of its desolate garden and barren trees. It was a long, flat stuccoed affair which might have been cheered by a coat of paint or whitewash, but nobody seemed to care about that and the shabby woodwork and rusty downspouts added to the general atmosphere of sadness and despair.

Knell had, from his boundless fund of local information, already given Littlejohn some details about the inhabitants.

'Kincaid, the village constable, says they live alone. No servants. They never seem to have visitors, not even tradesmen. The woman does their shopping at a little store in the village and collects the papers every day as she's out horseback riding. Now and then, if they need a plumber or a joiner, he's admitted, but they keep an eye on him all the time he's doing the job. The man who reads the electric meters calls, too, but Kincaid says he's in and out without seeing what goes on indoors.'

'Kincaid seems to be a very diligent officer.'

'In a small village, news travels fast and if they can't find a reason or an explanation for anything, they make one up. News about your coming here got around before you'd even arrived, and Kincaid said that, as you were from London, the murder of Joss Varran must have international connections.'

Before they could knock on the door, a figure appeared from round the corner of the house. A tall, stooping, heavily built man, dark and with a black beard, in corduroy trousers and an open-necked shirt. He wore a battered felt hat. He was carrying a bucket, a large sponge and a fistful of dusters. He paused and looked them up and down.

'You're Inspector Knell, aren't you?'

'Yes.'

'They said you were about.'

'Who did?'

'In the village. Everybody's on about Joss Varran's murder.'

'I've seen you before, haven't I?'

'Yes. I've seen you, too. At funerals. I'm the church grave-digger. Name's Quantrell.'

'What are you doing here?'

'Odd jobs. Aren't enough funerals to keep me alive. I do a bit for the forestry board, but that's only casual and doesn't bring in enough. I married a young wife late in life and we've two kids.'

Quantrell seemed set to give the fullest particulars of his personal finances and anything else they cared to know. He was, after all, earning five shillings an hour and talking was the best way of passing the time.

'Have you been cleaning the car?'

'Yes. It's standing round the corner. Come and take a look. It's a museum piece.'

It was too. An old Bentley touring model shining with bright brass. It must have been around fifty years old.

And E. D. Cojeen had told them that Joss Varran's last journey home had been made in a vintage Bentley.

'Who drives this?'

'The Colonel mostly did, until he got sick and couldn't trust himself to drive any more. He's very proud of it. Says he used to join in all the rallies when he was in England. It's a fine car. Better than many of these fancy new ones.'

'Who services it?'

'I do. My father used to be a blacksmith and I used to drive the steam roller for the highway board. Then they changed from steam to diesel oil and the fumes got on me chest. So I packed it up.'

Knell blinked at the list of qualifications.

'And that makes you able to act as mechanic for the old Bentley.'

'I've had it in pieces and put it together again. The Colonel played hell but he had to admit that it ran better after.'

Littlejohn coughed to remind Knell that they had work to do. The encounter between Knell and Quantrell was developing into what the Manx call a *li'l cooish*, an interminable exchange of news.

Knell then introduced Littlejohn and the ex-steam rollerman.

'Anybody at home in the manor?' asked Littlejohn.

'The Colonel's in, but you'll have to let me tell him you're here. He's cleaning the brasses and you'll have to give him time to move the brasses and change his workin' clothes. He doesn't like it if he's caught doing housework.'

'Is Miss Sarah at home?'

'She's out riding in the curraghs. She'll be back shortly. The Colonel will be wanting his tea and he won't do any cookin', so she's got to be back.'

'You'd better tell him we're here, then.'

'What if he won't see you?'

'Tell him it's the police.'

'That'll shake him, won't it? Is he suspected, then?'

'Just tell him we're here.'

Quantrell went inside and closed the door behind him. It was a good five minutes before he returned. He must have been persuading the colonel that he'd better see the police.

'Come this way.'

They found themselves in a large hall with very little in it. A hat-stand, a chair, a Persian rug on the floor, and not much else. A wide staircase rose from the back of the hall. Like the outside, everything had a moth-eaten look.

Quantrell opened a door to the left and indicated by a motion of his head that they might enter and then he left them.

The room was large and had broad windows overlooking the neglected garden. This, too, was sparsely furnished. A few chairs scattered about, two arm-chairs in front of an anthracite stove burning in the fireplace, which was of stone, spacious, and with a coat of arms of some kind or another on the keystone. A small dining table, a sideboard, and a grandfather clock ticking in one corner. It might have been that the occupants had arrived without much furniture and had bought their bare requirements in auction rooms.

Duffy was sitting in one of the arm-chairs, his legs stretched out to the fire. He did not rise to his feet but merely turned in the direction of the newcomers.

'Come in.'

He looked anything but an army man. Judging from the short legs stretched to the stove, he was small. Round faced, with a mottled purple complexion fading to an unhealthy yellow under his ears, thin white hair carefully parted and brushed across a low forehead, and a small clipped moustache. He was wearing an old tweed suit and looked to have settled himself in his present posture to meet his questioners. There was a tray with a bottle of whisky, a syphon and a half-filled glass at his elbow on a small table.

'I gather you're the police and wish to see me. What's it all about?'

He raised his bushy eyebrows and disclosed his pale expressionless eyes. Otherwise, he showed little interest. Then he looked at Littlejohn suspiciously.

'You're not from these parts.'

Knell interposed to introduce Littlejohn and himself.

'Scotland Yard. Good God! What's been happening and how does it concern me?'

'As you know, sir there's been a crime at Close Dhoo. Joss Varran, your near neighbour, was murdered the other night.'

'Quantrell did mention it I won't be much help to you. I didn't even know the fellow.'

'Are you sure? We've been informed that he was seen about this place last year.'

'Last year? That's a long time ago and in any case, whatever he came for was no concern of mine. Probably called to see Quantrell about something. You're barking up the wrong tree if you think I had anything to do with the crime. Why the hell are you pestering me about it?'

He fumbled in his pocket, produced a cigarette case, fumbled in that and then lit a cigarette.

'I'm not well and came here for a bit of peace and quiet. I don't want bothering by the police or anybody else about things that don't concern me. As for getting involved with Scotland Yard, the thing's preposterous. Why choose me to harass with your enquiries ... ?'

He got no further for they were disturbed by the arrival outside of a woman on horseback. She dismounted, handed the reins to Quantrell, who pointed to the house and said a few words, presumably about the arrival of the police, and strode indoors.

'My niece is here. You'd better ask her, although she knows as little as I do.'

His niece! First his wife, then his daughter, and some had said his mistress. It seemed true that when country folk couldn't find an answer to a situation, they made one up.

She came right in without any delay or preamble. She was not in the least disconcerted by their presence and gazed steadily at them.

'What's going on here?'

It was quite certain that whenever she entered a room, the rest of the people and contents were, momentarily, at least, forgotten. She was tall, well built and strong, and confident. She was dark, like a gypsy, with fine features and a passionate mouth and clear brown eyes. The sort who would bring philanderers like Joss Varran eagerly in her wake and, judging from her apparent annoyance at the intruders, deal with them suitably.

Knell explained the purpose of their visit just as he had done to her uncle.

She ignored him and confined herself to Littlejohn, whom she judged at once was the higher authority.

'I expect this is a door-to-door excursion in search of information. I can tell you right away that this sordid little affair is no concern of ours and you must leave my uncle in peace. He is unwell and is in this remote place for the benefit of his health. He must not be disturbed.'

'There are one or two questions we wish to ask you and then we'll trouble you both no further ... '

'I'm surprised at you, Chief Superintendent, traipsing round the countryside, wasting your valuable time, on a crime which has obviously been committed by some vagrant or other for the sake of a few pounds ... '

'Excuse me, Miss Duffy, but what I do with my time is no affair of yours. Inspector Knell is a personal friend of mine, and I'm helping him with a case about which you seem to know much more than your uncle, who says he knows nothing at all about it and apparently cares less. Now, will you listen to me and be reasonable. You seem to be causing the commotion, not us. If you and your uncle will quietly answer what we have to ask, we'll leave you in peace ... '

Her initial fit of temper seemed to leave her and she quietened down.

'Very well. Be brief then. What do you wish to know?'

'Did you know the victim, Joss Varran?'

'Why should we? He was a near neighbour but we didn't associate with him. As a matter of fact, we couldn't if we'd wished to. Until the day of the crime, he was in gaol and had been there for over a year.'

'You seem well informed about his movements?'

'All the information is in the newspapers. Do you wish me to produce them and show you?'

'No. Presumably your uncle isn't as interested in such news as you are.'

She bit her lip angrily.

'Please get on ...'

'We're informed that before he left and was put in gaol he was seen around this house. Can you explain that?'

'He certainly didn't come here at our invitation, nor did we see him. He must have been after Quantrell for something.'

'Perhaps we'd better have Quantrell in and ask him ...'

'You will do no such thing. You can interrogate him on your way out, which I hope will be very soon.'

'You have a Bentley car, I believe. What one would call a vintage model?'

'Yes. It was a hobby of my uncle's when he was in better health.'

Littlejohn turned to the Colonel.

'You still drive it?'

He did not reply, but left it to his niece, who seemed by now fully in charge of the situation.

'He does, now and then, when he feels better. What has that to do with the crime?'

'On the night he died, Joss Varran, making his way to Close Dhoo after dark, was picked up and given a lift by someone in an old Bentley car. Probably the owner was the last person to see him alive, except his murderer.'

Duffy fumbled for another cigarette.

'It wasn't me, I can assure you.'

'Where were you both on that night?'

Sarah Duffy was quick to reply.

'It was not our car. There are other vintage cars on the Island. As for where we were, we were here. My uncle was unwell and I stayed indoors with him from after tea until bedtime.'

'Neither of you went out after tea until the following morning?'

'That is what I said. We have nobody else to give us an alibi. This is a remote place and other people are hardly likely to wander about in these bogs after dark. In any case, why should we produce an alibi? This is no affair of ours.'

'You are neighbours of the Varrans. I can see the chimney of the cottage through the window from where I'm standing now. It is natural that we should ask if you saw anything unusual going on there of late.'

'I told you we were not interested in Varran. Or in his house or what he did there.'

'We're mainly interested in what he did *here*. We have it on good authority that he was seen about this house before he went to gaol.'

'We've already told you we know nothing about any such visits. Quantrell may know. And now, if you don't mind, I wish to prepare tea and I think, too, that my uncle has been worried quite enough. So, good afternoon…'

There seemed no point in persisting, so Littlejohn and Knell bade them good day and the Duffys hadn't even the grace to show them to the door. As they let themselves out, they met Quantrell again. This time he was entering the main gate on a ramshackle old motor bicycle.

'I'm just bringin' in the milk…'

He indicated a small metal milk can swinging from his handlebars.

'…We don't have a milkman delivering here. I fetch it from Close-e-Cass about half a mile down the road.'

Littlejohn nodded.

'The Candell place?'

'That's right. You know them, then?'

'Yes. Isabel Varran went to them for help after she found her brother's dead body.'

'I'd forgotten ... Nasty business.'

'Did you know him?'

'Not particularly. Certainly not lately. He'd been in gaol up to the time he was killed. Before that, I used to see him around. Never had anything to do with him.'

'That's strange ... '

Littlejohn lit his pipe to allow his comment to sink in.

'What's strange?'

For the first time, Quantrell's good humour seemed to leave him.

'We've been told that before he went away and got himself put in prison, he was seen about this place.'

'Who told you that? I'll bet it was old Candell up in his tower, spying on the locality through his field glasses.'

'But he wasn't the only one. What have you to say about that?'

Quantrell gave him a sly wink.

'I know all about it. Joss Varran was a one for the ladies and his fancy ran high just before he went to gaol. He tried to make the acquaintance of Miss Sarah. He didn't come and knock on the door of the manor, although he'd cheek enough. He used to hang around, all toffed up, trying to meet Miss Sarah when she was out riding. He didn't succeed, though. She rode past him and if he'd persisted, I'm damn sure she'd have run him down. He came twice with a trumped up tale about seed potatoes and asked me if I'd got any for sale. He asked a question or two about the Colonel and then about Miss Sarah, but he didn't get much change out of me. I told him I was busy and that the Colonel would be annoyed if he found him around the place.'

'I see. And that's the only connection he had with you all.'

'That's right.'

'What time do you leave here at night?'

'Around five. Why?'

'You don't happen to know if the Colonel or Miss Sarah was out on the night Varran died? You see, that night Joss Varran got a lift home from Ramsey in an old Bentley.'

'Have you asked them at the house?'

'Yes. They said they were indoors all night.'

'Well?'

'I was just checking. They might have forgotten.'

Quantrell sniggered.

'Was it after dark?'

'Yes.'

'They weren't out then. They never go out in the Bentley after dark. It's wired for night use, but I've never known them take it out. On the rare occasions they do go out after dark, they send for a taxi from the village. I'd have known if the big car was out that night. I look after it and I'd know if it had been used by the state it was in. You follow?'

'Yes. Are there any similar cars in the vicinity?'

'I couldn't say. There must be, surely. They hold vintage car rallies sometimes. I'm not much interested in old crocks, except the Colonel's Bentley and that because I have to clean it and keep it in good condition.'

'How long have you worked for them?'

'Ever since they came here. About three years.'

He looked uneasy.

'I'd better be off. Miss Sarah will be wanting the milk for tea and she'll have the skin off me if it's not there when she's ready for it.'

He remounted and wobbled away to the house with some difficulty, for the bike was coughing badly.

As the two policemen made for the gate, they saw that the Colonel had now found his feet and was watching them anxiously through the window.

'What do we know about Quantrell and his background, Knell?' Littlejohn asked on the way back to the village. 'Is he a Manxman?'

'The name has a bit of a Manx sound about it, but the man's voice ... He has a Liverpool flavour to me. Perhaps we could find out. Shall we see if P.C. Kincaid is available?'

Kincaid wasn't. A visitor had dropped dead in his precinct and he'd gone to sort things out for the inquest.

A few doors away from the police station there was a small store, a converted house, modest compared with the larger ones of the village which had grown with the population, but obviously still well patronised judging from the stock on the shelves. Over the door a simple notice. *A. Kinvig.*

Knell excused himself to Littlejohn.

'I just want a packet of cigarettes ... '

He entered the shop. It was empty and he got a warm welcome from the polite little apple-cheeked woman behind the clean worn counter.

'Well, well. Reggie Knell. What brings you here?'

They exchanged friendly greetings. When he was a boy, Knell's uncle had farmed in Scroundal, not far away, and he had always spent a part of his summer holidays there. Amy was his own age and they had played together. Her widowed mother had then owned the shop and Amy had inherited it on her death.

Knell had a slight feeling of claustrophobia in the crowded little stores. Racks on three sides filled with tinned goods, bottles of toffee, packages of food, spools of thread, and in one corner a small dispensary of patent medicines for counteracting and curing the effects of the foods. Knell leaned, talking, with his elbow on a food refrigerator in which he could see frozen sausages, fish and steak pies. He asked for his cigarettes and Amy produced them from under the counter.

'Do you know a man called Quantrell, Amy?'

Her tongue clicked against her teeth.

'Has he been up to something again?'

'Why? Does he often get in trouble with the police?'

'Nothing serious, really. He gets drunk now and then and he's always awkward when he's had too much. And he runs an old motor bike and gets in trouble for dangerous driving...'

'How long has he lived in the village?'

'About three years. He was born on the Island. I think it was at Cronk-y-Voddey. His father was a blacksmith and Mr. Quantrell served with his father for a bit and then he went across and got a job as an engineer in Liverpool. There was some trouble, nobody seems to know what it was, and he came back here to live and got a job driving the roller on the roads. He gave that up and now does odd jobs, like digging graves when the sexton's sciatica is troubling him. He does gardening, too, at Ballakee Manor.'

'He's married?'

'Yes, with two children, but he's so awkward when the drink is in him that his wife's left him and gone to live with her mother in Douglas.'

'And he's living alone?'

'Yes, in a cottage at the head of Ballaugh Glen.'

'Did he know Joss Varran, Amy?'

She caught her breath.

'Is that what's brought you here, Reggie?'

'Yes. But you won't tell a soul that I've been making enquiries, will you, Amy?'

'Of course not, if you say so.'

He knew he could trust her, although all the gossip of the village and beyond was passed around the shop along with the tinned goods and frozen puddings and fish.

'What a pity about Joss. We're all sorry for poor Isabel. But I don't think Joss and Mr. Quantrell were friendly. They may have met in the pub. Joss was always in there whenever he was at home and Mr. Quantrell was one of the regulars, too. Joss, of course, was away for a long time, wasn't he?'

Knell admired her polite, discreet manner. The way she called Quantrell 'Mister' and how she avoided giving Joss the stigma of prison.

Customers were beginning to arrive and it wouldn't do to start the ball of gossip rolling, so Knell bade Amy good-bye and she gave him a conspiratorial look to assure him that his secrets were safe.

When Knell told Littlejohn what he'd learned, Littlejohn wished there were a few more little stores and women like Amy scattered around London to supplement so easily the records of Scotland Yard.

Chapter VII
The Shaking Field

As littlejohn and Knell were leaving the village, they passed Kincaid in his official vehicle and Knell signalled to him to stop. Then he called through the window to him to proceed to the police station where they would meet him and discuss the case so far. They could very well have talked by the roadside, but Knell, who was panting for his afternoon cup of tea, had a crafty idea that Kincaid's hospitable Manx wife would provide what he needed without even the asking.

Kincaid's official headquarters were in the front room of his house, a modestly equipped place with a desk, some cupboards, two chairs and a counter between himself and the public to define the status of Law and suppliant. Framed photographs of Her Majesty and Sir Winston Churchill on the walls together with a lot of official notices and edicts.

P.C. Kincaid was a young constable, very civil and intelligent, knew his place, but wasn't intimidated by his superiors, married to a nice wife and he had two young children. He was delighted to meet Littlejohn and to be officially drawn into the investigation of which, hitherto, he had merely hovered on the fringe. Excusing himself, he went in the rear quarters to bring in another chair and at the same time managed to pass a message to his wife about refreshments and to his offspring about behaving themselves during the visit of the V.I.P.s in the front room.

In a very short time, Mrs. Kincaid arrived, towing behind her a trolley containing scones, soda cakes, tea and home-made gingerbread and, after being introduced and passing round the good things, withdrew and left them to their business.

Kincaid was a well-built man with a fresh complexion, a dominant nose of almost Wellingtonian proportions and a humorous mouth and eyes. His superiors said he would go far, which was his wife's independent opinion, too, for she was very proud of him. He was a good gardener in his spare time and in a cabinet in the living-room reposed various cups he'd won at horticultural shows all over the Island.

Knell briefly filled in the picture of the case so far, and was rather surprised to find that Kincaid knew as much as he did about it all. He definitely didn't like Quantrell.

'He's a bit of a mystery and a liar as well. If the Duffys needed an alibi, he'd give them one if they paid him for it. As for his not knowing much about Joss Varran, they were both regulars at the village pub and were often in one another's company there before Joss got gaoled. I have to keep an eye on Quantrell. He drinks too much and gets noisy when he's drunk. And he runs an old motor-bike that's a menace on the roads.'

'You've formed your own ideas about who might have killed Joss Varran, Kincaid?' Littlejohn asked him.

'No, I haven't, sir. I know what goes on in my patch, and I'm sure nobody would go so far as to kill him. He was an unpleasant fellow, a heavy drinker, fond of the women ... But, in my opinion, he hadn't, before he left and got himself in prison, sufficiently offended anybody in these parts to make them run the risk of murdering him. What he did when he was away from here was another matter. It might be anybody, elsewhere on the Island or on the mainland. I might be prejudiced, but in my view we can write off any of the locals...'

'What about Quantrell?'

'If he'd done it, he'd have cleared off and left the Island right away. He's still got connections in England. I know that because from time to time he goes across. I could never find out what he did when he went to England. I'd very much like to know what it was. He's a wife and two children and he doesn't keep them on what he earns by odding about at the manor or digging an occasional grave here. He never seems short of money.'

'You'd better keep an eye on him. He and Varran might have been up to something and quarrelled about it. By the way, Colonel Duffy owns a vintage Bentley. Does Quantrell ever drive it? As we've told you, Varran got a lift from Ramsey in an old Bentley on the night he died.'

'And the Duffys said they were indoors all that night, sir. Yes. If he thought he'd take the Bentley out, Quantrell has cheek enough to do it. The colonel wouldn't sack him for it. Who would he get to do what Quantrell does at the manor if he lost him? Such labour is hard to get here, especially when Quantrell is quite skilled at odd jobs and the Duffys don't care for other visitors at their place. Quantrell can turn his hand to plumbing, joinering, motor mechanic's jobs... No; they wouldn't sack him for using the car on the quiet, even if they found out, which, knowing Quantrell's cunning, is unlikely.'

'We'd better have as much information as possible about the people at the manor, Knell; the Colonel, Sarah, and Quantrell. I think you'd better get your people on the job of tracing their past records and movements. As far as I can see, there's not much use in repeating today's visit and interrogating the lot of them again. They'll only tell us what they wish us to know and the rest will presumably be a pack of lies.'

'I'll see to it, sir.'

And he gave Kincaid instructions to telephone head-quarters right away and set in motion the matter of records.

'...And when you've done that, Kincaid, come and join us at Close Dhoo,' said Knell. 'We've left the Archdeacon there and he may have some information for us after he's interviewed Isabel Varran.'

'I don't envy him his job, sir. When I tried to take a state-ment from her and arrange for her to identify her broth-er's body, she seemed thoroughly mixed up. She's a queer, lonely sort and never has much to say for herself. I found her completely incoherent. I'd to guess at most of what she was saying.'

'The Archdeacon will probably do better. He's an expert at extracting confessions...'

'You don't mean that you suspect her?'

'No, no. I was speaking in general terms. We'll see you at Close Dhoo, then.'

And after thanking Mrs. Kincaid for her hospitality, somewhat to her confusion, they left for the curraghs again.

They found the Archdeacon placidly enjoying his tea with Isabel. She had brought out what remained of her mother's best tea set and asked the newcomers to join them. They thanked her and told her of their meal at the police station, but said a cup of tea wouldn't come amiss and as they enjoyed it, the Archdeacon recited briefly what Isabel had told him.

As for Isabel, she seemed completely changed. The opportunity of telling her story quietly and in her own way to a sympathetic listener had done her a lot of good and she even smiled now and then.

It was quite clear that Isabel knew very little of any use to them in the investigation. Except that interest had been focused on the Shaking Field with its hiding place in the bog.

Littlejohn said he thought they ought to investigate it right away.

'Do you know exactly where the spot is, Miss Varran? Old Mr. Candell at Close-e-Cass knows it, because he told us that from the tower in which he lives, he could see that the place had been disturbed but it will be as well to check it if you have the information.'

The family Bible was produced again, but the map in the end was not detailed enough. The Archdeacon had an idea.

'You have the title to this house, Isabel?'

'Yes. It's up the chimney. Shall I get it down?'

She produced without trouble the biscuit tin in which her treasures were hidden and the Archdeacon found the necessary papers from among the rest. He read the deed cursorily.

'There's a clause here giving the owner of this house the right to a spade's cutting of turf at the statutory period for turf gathering.'

He chuckled.

'Someone is going to have a task here, if we can't get more details. If my memory serves me right, the traditional definition of a spade's cutting is sixty yards, by two yards and twenty-seven inches depth! So, it would appear that we'd better consult old Junius Candell after all. Wait a minute, though…'

On one corner of the back of the deed was written in faded ink, in an illiterate hand, '*dhrine. fore paces in.*'

'Someone has apparently scribbled this brief description as a reminder of where the hiding place was made. *Dhrine* is Manx for thorn bush. It's worth a trial. Have you a spade, Isabel?'

'Yes; there's one in the shed. I'll get it.'

She left them, not quite understanding what it was all about and where it was leading to, and returned with the spade.

'You'll please excuse it being so dirty. Somebody's been using it and didn't clean it when it was put away. I always clean it myself after I use it. It stops it from rusting and it lasts longer. I can't think…'

She paused.

'Had Joss been diggin'?'

Her question remained unanswered, for Kincaid had just arrived outside in his official car and was briskly parking it behind Knell's vehicle. His appearance caused considerable relief, especially to Knell, who was anticipating some vigorous work with the spade in the bog. He gave Kincaid a brief outline of the task before them.

'I well remember my grandfather had some turf rights in the Jurby curraghs, but I never went there with him. He used a special sort of spade to cut the peat…'

Kincaid pointed at the one Knell was offering him.

'You need a special sort of spade for turf; that kind won't do.'

'It will have to do; there's no other. And in any case, we're not cutting peat, we're digging in it.'

They formed a small procession, the Archdeacon leading the way, because he knew the bearings and details. Isabel seemed curious and asked if she might join them.

'The best way in is through the back. That's the road my father went when he hid his things in the curragh.'

They filed through the depressing back garden and through a break in the hedge at the end of the rough path until they found themselves overlooking a small barren field which seemed to have resisted all attempts at drainage and cultivation. There was a pond in one corner and the water from it had seeped into most of the top-soil and converted it into a marsh. It was surrounded by neglected hedges as though at some time someone had been anxious to enclose and segregate it from the surrounding fertile land. This, according to the Archdeacon's reading of the primitive map, was the Creelagh, or Shaking Land.

'Who owns this nowadays?' the Archdeacon asked Isabel Varran, who had put on a pair of old gumboots and was watching the proceedings with puzzled interest.

'I don't know. It's been like this as long as I can remember. Nobody ever seems to have worked it or put cattle on it. Not that it would grow or feed anything. It's what they call rotten land.'

There was a gap in the neglected hedge near where they were standing; probably there had once been a gate there of which nothing now remained. They made their way through it. Running the length of the hedge was a spine of land higher than the rest, and dry.

The Archdeacon walked along it and the others followed. He seemed to be talking to himself.

'Junius Candell talked of being able to see the spot which had been disturbed from his tower. We can't see the tower from here and, therefore, we'd better find the place where it is visible. It lies, I think, in that direction...'

He pointed to where a belt of twisted trees obscured whatever was beyond. They continued their walk until a gap in the screen revealed the roof of Close-e-Cass with the tower dominating it.

'This might be somewhere near the spot.'

They closely examined it. The skin of the turf, the top sod, dry and rough with ling, had obviously been disturbed, but whoever had done so had carefully replaced it.

'This is roughly four paces in, as the note says on the deed, but the thorn bush, the dhrine, seems to have gone long ago. Let's try digging here, Kincaid.'

P.C. Kincaid removed his tunic.

'Hold that for me,' he said, handing it to Isabel.

He tackled the job with vigour, first flinging off the top soil and skin, then striking the compact peat about a foot down. Kincaid paused and rested on his spade.

'This part's been disturbed. See? It's not been put back carefully like the top sod.'

He continued with his work, which was now more difficult as he hit the solid peat, which, under the spade, cut like a piece of cake. Finally, at a depth of around two feet, he struck something solid.

'We ought to have brought Quantrell with us. He's got the knack of digging graves. By the feel of it, we've struck a coffin or something...'

More spade-work in the hole he'd created revealed a kind of lid made of solid, roughly dressed wood. It took a lot more effort on the part of Kincaid finally to clear it of turf and bring to light the whole of it, which covered a cavity about a yard square. Then, using his spade as a lever, he removed part of the loose lid. He worked very gingerly, for beneath him he found a compartment almost a yard deep. Knell handed him his pocket torch and Kincaid examined the queer receptacle.

'There's a lot of old stuff down here ... Rusty pipes and a funny thing like a little wash-boiler ... '

The contents presented a problem. Not only was Kincaid's uniform suffering from his manoeuvres in the peat, but he couldn't secure a proper foothold to enable him to get at and remove the contents of the queer box.

'We'd better get some help and tackle for this job,' said Knell. 'What about calling in Baz and Joe Candell?'

He looked at Littlejohn for an answer.

'That's right, Knell. Tell them to bring some ropes and come in old clothes. They'll need more spades, too. And whilst you're at the farm, try to get a word with old Junius Candell. He said he'd seen from his tower that this turf had been disturbed. At that distance, even with a first-rate pair of binoculars, he could never have spotted that; the top turf was too carefully replaced. How did he know there'd been digging going on here and did he see anyone doing it?'

They all made off for the house again and Isabel brewed some more tea whilst Knell drove away for help.

Knell, was not away for long and returned in company with Baz and Joe. The Candell men were shy in such company and it was obvious that they had not quite understood the purpose for which they had been brought there. They had their spades with them, although the idea of digging in the bog seemed futile to them. They presented a sharp contrast. Baz, who had a reputation for being all brawn and little brain, was tall and beefy, with a pleasant smile and full of good nature. He was round-faced and ruddy and his hair was clipped short, for he was thrifty and believed in getting his money's worth when he visited the barber. Joe was smaller and more wiry, with long hair growing down the back of his neck and sideburns, a thinner face than his brother's and a foxy look.

Knell at once took Littlejohn aside and in a low voice expressed his indignation at the reception old Junius Candell had given him.

'The old man and the girl, Beulah, are not on our side. Beulah hates Joss Varran so much that you'd think the murderer had done her a favour in killing him. She's venomous about him, and the old man, of course, who almost eats out of her hand, supports her. When I asked if I could see old Junius, Mrs. Candell went up the tower to ask him and he flatly refused. Said he wasn't well and not up to talking with the police. I didn't wish to press the matter and I got the impression that it wouldn't be any use if I did see him…'

'Awkward, but what one might expect. He's in his dotage.'

'…So, Mrs. Candell having told the Archdeacon that Beulah and Baz were great friends, I asked Baz to go and ask his sister about what she and old Junius saw going on at the Shaking Ground. The chief difficulty then was in getting Baz to understand what I wanted him to ask her. He was very willing to help and, finally, after we'd had a little rehearsal as to exactly what he must ask, he went aloft to the tower room and saw his sister. He was soon back. He'd had no difficulty. It seems Beulah and the old man saw what appeared to be the light of a flashlamp moving at the bog and old Junius said somebody was busy at the Shaking Ground. Next morning, they looked at the spot through their field glasses, which the old man uses very frequently, and Junius said there'd been somebody digging there. Either the view of the land from the tower is different and signs of digging are visible from there, which I doubt, or else he'd made it up to show Beulah how clever he was. That's the best I could do.'

'At least, it explains the information he gave us about the land. We'd better get busy now, or it will be dark before we've finished.'

The procession made its way back to the bog, including Isabel, who seemed to be burning with curiosity. On the way, she and Baz indulged in pleasant conversation, a pair of simple people who understood one another and had no inhibitions when they were together.

They arrived at the spot which the Archdeacon now described as Kincaid's Hole. There Baz and Joe, slow and methodical, as became experts in the handling of land, surveyed the scene. Then they examined the hole itself as though appraising Kincaid's amateur workmanship. They both seemed astonished at the contents.

'Some sort of drainage engine?' asked Joe.

'We think it's an old still that Michael Varran hid there.'

Baz, who found it hard to understand any new idea, looked incredulous.

'Still what?'

Knell patiently tried to explain.

'A still for making whisky.'

'Whisky? Go on!'

Baz thought it was a joke.

'I'll tell you later, Baz. The job now is to enlarge the hole, so that you can get down and hand out the contents.'

Baz and Joe sized up the amount of further excavation required and having decided between them, set to work with the easy skill of professional performers with a spade.

It did not take them long and soon they were in a position to handle what looked like a lot of old iron. Baz allowed Joe to do this, as Joe was less bulky and more nimble for the job. He groped about in the hole, handed his finds to Baz, who passed them to Knell who stood on the edge. First came a rusty boiler, with a tight-fitting lid from which protruded a pipe, like an arm. The boiler was quite empty.

'What's all this?' said Baz, who made up in extreme curiosity what he lacked in brains. 'Looks like a washin' day.'

Knell gingerly relieved Baz of his burden and laid it down.

'This is what's called a whisky still, Baz. It's illegal to distil whisky and that's why Michael Varran took so much trouble to hide all this. If you want to make it, you boil up fermented liquor in the boiler, which is called a retort, and the vapour comes out at the pipe you see here...'

Baz tried to look as if he understood what was being said, but he was befuddled by Knell's confused lecture.

'Come on, Baz. Take a hold of this.'

Joe was offering his brother another queer find; a coiled tube, covered in verdigris. Baz passed it on to Knell.

'This is called the "worm". When you're distilling, it's surrounded or submerged in water to keep it cool, and the spirit emerges from it drop by drop.'

Baz was filled with admiration at Knell's knowledge.

'Have you ever made the whisky, Mr. Knell?'

'Didn't I tell you it's illegal. We have a book at the police station that explains all about it. As far as I know, there isn't any poteen made in the Isle of Man. Poteen's another word for whisky. But we have to know about these things, just in case anybody tried it.'

'That's all,' said Joe, dishevelled and grimy from his efforts.

Knell's face fell and the Candells exchanged looks of disgust. It was as if all three of them had expected to unearth a buried treasure or, at least, something more interesting than a lot of old iron.

'Have you seen this equipment before, Miss Varran?'

She looked at Littlejohn and shook her head.

'No. As I said, my dad used to keep it all secret. Nobody was allowed in the kitchen when he was boilin'. That must have been the boiler that he used.'

Joe climbed from the hole and Knell leaned over and examined the empty cavity by the light of his torch.

'What's that in the corner, there?'

Joe looked up from dusting himself down.

'What?'

'There's a little white thing. Looks like a pencil, or something.'

Joe laboriously lowered himself in the peat again and groped about where Knell had indicated. Then he handed Knell what he had found.

It was a white cheap ball-point pen, which Knell passed on to Littlejohn.

'That's not much use to us. There are thousands of them in circulation. It might be anybody's.'

'That's right, Knell, but it proves that this hiding place has been opened since Michael Varran hid away his still for the last time. Little gimmicks like this weren't in existence in those days.'

Isabel Varran took the pen from Littlejohn's hand and examined it.

'This is mine. I wondered where it had got to. I thought I'd lost it. It disappeared about the last time Joss was at home before he went to prison. He must have taken it. It must have dropped out of his pocket when he was digging here. But what was he wantin' here?'

They all wondered that.

Chapter VIII
A Man of Initiative

There Seemed no sense in leaving the excavation in the Shaking Field wide open and Knell instructed the Candells to fill it in, smooth down the surface and restore it to the state in which they had found it. He got the impression that this displeased Joe and Baz, who probably wished to bring friends there on a tour of inspection, when they could exhibit their finds and explain, in a fashion, the mysteries of poteen making and Michael Varran's illegal indulgence in it years ago.

After that, the party broke up, to the further disappointment of Joe and Baz, who obviously, somehow arising from the discovery of the still, expected an arrest to be made right away. It was growing dark as Littlejohn, the Archdeacon and Knell started for Grenaby. The curraghs surrounding Close Dhoo had a sad, haunted look in the last of the daylight and the tumbledown, empty houses, once thronged with children and their old-fashioned parents, added to the depression like uneasy, forgotten dreams. Very different from Grenaby when they reached it. The dying village has suddenly sprung to life again as families fleeing from the taxes and turmoil of the mainland, had found refuge there, renovated and occupied the once empty cottages, and joined the Archdeacon's flock. The houses which, when first Littlejohn had known the place, had been black and forlorn after dark, were now illuminated and the activities of their occupants seemed to have driven away the traditional monsters, bugganes and fenodyrees which infested the place by night.

Maggie Keggin met them at the door and gave Knell her usual hearty welcome.

'Why don't you bring your bed?'

There were prawns to begin with; then Manx salmon; followed by apple tart and whipped cream, and Stilton cheese. Until the port arrived, they were not allowed to discuss crime. Then, the table was quickly cleared, for Maggie Keggin was following a serial on television and was eager for the next instalment. As she left them, she handed Knell an envelope addressed to him.

'A policeman in a van brought this just after you arrived back. I kept it from you because you'd only have opened it and spoiled the dinner by reading the contents over your meal.'

Knell chucked her under the chin.

'And don't take liberties with me, Reginald Knell. You're not in Douglas now.'

All the same, she left them looking pleased.

Knell opened the official envelope Maggie had given him. It contained several sheets of typescript.

The island police had been busy. From a firm of Ramsey estate agents they had learned that Colonel Christopher Duffy had leased Ballakee Manor for three years. He had paid his rent quarterly by cheque on a Ramsey bank. Sponsored by the same estate agents, Duffy had opened his banking account on his arrival in Ramsey. The police had questioned the bank manager.

The bank had been a bit cagey, as usual, when asked about the account and particularly about Duffy's income. The manager confessed, however, that they never received any warrants for army pension from the Colonel.

'I'll bet he isn't a colonel at all,' said Knell. 'He's just helped himself to the rank and title.'

The police memorandum continued with exemplary thoroughness. They had persisted in asking for the source of Duffy's income. The account was fed, it appeared by cash in one pound notes. The Colonel had mentioned casually that he made quite a nice little income from horse racing. 'I've friends at some of the mainland stables.'

In the course of general conversation with the estate agent's clerk the police had learned that Duffy had won first prize with his vintage car in the *cours d'élégance* class at a rally in the Island two years ago. The clerk had mentioned that his picture had appeared along with winners in other classes in the local paper. The police had thereupon visited the local paper and obtained prints of the photographs, which not only showed Duffy but also Sarah Duffy at his side. Luckily they'd removed their goggles. And, in the crowd in the background was the attendant mechanic, Quantrell.

'Splendid! Splendid!' rejoiced Knell. 'Now we can circulate their pictures and find out if they're known anywhere.'

'Where do you circulate them?' asked the Archdeacon. 'All over the British Isles and beyond?'

'It says here that the estate agents told our men that Duffy stayed at a Ramsey hotel and contacted them from there. Our men enquired at the hotel and were told that Duffy didn't write for rooms, but booked-in casually. However, a couple of letters had been forwarded from his previous address. The hotel manager said he could only remember the name of the place; he'd forgotten the rest, if he ever knew it. "They were re-addressed from Ribchester, near Preston".'

'You'd better contact the Preston police, then, Knell, and enquire if Duffy and his woman have ever crossed their path. Anything else?'

'Nothing about Quantrell from Liverpool yet. And Scotland Yard are trying to contact Joss Varran's cellmates in the Scrubs. That's all so far.'

They then discussed the day's work and its implications.

Before his spell in gaol, Joss Varran had spent very little time at home and had been employed as a deckhand on a container ferry plying between Preston and Ramsey, with occasional trips to London.

'We ought to have a talk with the captain about Varran's character and movements,' said Littlejohn, and Knell made a note of it. 'Was he with shipmates when the fight blew up in London?'

'I'll enquire when the boat's due to dock in Ramsey and we can see the captain then.'

'And if the men who were with Varran when the police hauled them off for violence, are still members of the crew, we'd better get to know exactly what happened that night.'

'According to the records, Varran returned to the Isle of Man as soon as he was released from the Scrubs. Why the hurry, I wonder? His sister implied that he wasn't a home-bird. Let's assume the reason was that Varran had something, probably cash, stowed away in his hiding place in the Shaking Field. He made for it as soon as possible and presumably removed it before he started for home. In recovering whatever he'd hidden, he dropped the ball-point pen from his pocket. He was killed after leaving the bog by someone who had followed him there. Was the murderer after what Varran had recovered from the cache in the peat?'

Knell scribbled a note of it in his book.

'And don't let's forget,' he said, 'that Isabel Varran said that she couldn't find his kit-bag when she looked for it. Perhaps he put whatever he dug up in the kit-bag and the murderer carried it off, bag and all.'

The Archdeacon filled his pipe again and lit it.

'And now we arrive at the murderer himself. He must have known what was hidden there...'

Littlejohn shook his head.

'Not *there*, perhaps, but somewhere. It must have been something worth following Varran for, maybe money. And Varran must have either confided in the murderer about its existence, or, at least, given some hint of it.'

'Could it have been one of his cell-mates in gaol?'

'...Or someone who knew of what was hidden, even before Varran went to gaol, and who waited patiently for his return.'

The Archdeacon turned to Knell.

'You have the dramatis personae of the case in your little book, Reginald. Let's run through it.'

Knell opened his notebook with enthusiasm, as though, at last, they had reached a practical stage in the case.

'Shall I deal with them one by one, as I entered them in my book as the case unfolded?'

'Yes. That's as good a way as any.'

'There's the Candells. Father, mother, two sons, Uncle Tom, Beulah and old Junius.'

'And they gave you a sort of composite alibi, Knell, didn't they, saying they were all in bed at the time of the crime?' said Littlejohn.

'That's right.'

'And yet, Junius Candell talked about seeing lights in the region of the Shaking Land that night. Presumably that was Joss Varran in search of his hiding place. We can pinpoint the time Junius saw it. E. D. Cojeen saw Joss taking a lift home in the Bentley at just after nine. Isabel Varran found the body at just after ten. How long would it take to get from Ramsey to Close Dhoo in a vintage car, Archdeacon?'

'That depends on the speed of travel, doesn't it?'

'Say, forty miles an hour. A vintage Bentley in good condition would do that easily...'

'Let's say twenty minutes,' said Knell.

'Wait! That's assuming Varran got a lift to the very door of Close Dhoo. Did old Candell say what time he saw the lights at the Shaking Field?'

'I asked Baz, who, you remember, was acting as go-between. He went back to the old man to enquire. He said he didn't know; but Beulah did. She said Junius, who usually goes to bed between nine and ten, had a whim that night to stay up and listen to the weather report on the radio at ten. She went up to his room at twenty to ten to bid him good night and found him at the window in his nightshirt. He said he was waiting for the report and she told him the time and said he'd better get in bed and wait for it there, as he'd get his death of cold wandering about ill-clad. He was persuaded to do that and told her then about the light in the curragh and she looked out and saw it.'

'Had the rest of the family retired then?'

'I asked Baz and he said yes. Beulah always went to bid her grandfather good night before she got in bed herself.'

'So, the family alibi might not be as tight as we thought. They weren't all asleep, at least. We'd better go to Close-e-Cass and make further enquiries.'

'You mean, one of them might have done it?'

'It isn't likely, but we must remember Baz was an enemy of Joss Varran.'

'All the same, how was Baz to know the exact time at which to waylay Joss? In any case, the timing is very close. Ramsey at nine, a car journey of twenty minutes, a walk from where Joss was put down, lights at his hiding place at nine-forty, dead at ten. It seems to indicate that he left the car somewhere very near the Shaking Field. The car may have dropped him either near his own home or, let's say, at the manor. It might have been the Duffys' car after all. The manor isn't far distant from the hiding place. You have the Duffys and Quantrell on your list, Knell?'

'Yes. We're waiting for information from Records about the three of them. We should know by morning.'

'What about Joss's cell-mates?'

'John Jukes, otherwise Cracker Jack, safebreaker, and Cliff Larkin, housebreaker. Both released a week or two before Joss. Their reports should be along soon, too.'

'It would seem that the Duffy pair are somehow involved. Was Joss acquainted with Sarah and was the Colonel jealous? Or were the lot of them, including Quantrell, in some illegal affair together?'

'We may find out when the reports reach us, though I doubt it, sir.'

'In whatever direction we cast our minds, we're faced with the mystery of the Shaking Field. What had Joss Varran hidden there and who else was connected with it? The truth is, Knell, we've not got enough information and background about the parties in the case.

'Tomorrow, we must set about obtaining it...'

Telephone.

'Who can that be at this hour?'

Maggie Keggin entered. She looked annoyed.

'A man to speak to Inspector Littlejohn on the telephone. He won't give his name and when I tried to insist, he got impertinent. I ought to have hung-up on him, but I thought it might be important.'

Littlejohn followed Maggie to the hall.

Without giving his name or any greeting the caller began to upbraid Littlejohn.

'...I'd have thought you would have at least had the courtesy to question me about the murder of Joss Varran. You ignored me during your visit this morning to Close-e-Cass and I believe you've been round the countryside interviewing all and sundry. After all, I'm the Varran family's representative. I've a right...'

'Just a minute, please. Who is that?'

'Sydney Handy, of Narradale. Brother-in-law of the deceased...'

'Have you some useful information to give the police, Mr. Handy?'

There was a pause. The question had taken the wind from Sydney's sails and he was groping in his mind for an excuse.

'Yes!'

'What is it?'

'I've been speakin' with Kincaid, the local constable, about Joss's belongings. He showed me a list, but wouldn't hand anything over. There was his knife, his watch, his cigarettes and matches, a dirty handkerchief and two pieces of string, half-a-crown and two threepenny bits in change, and his old wallet with his sailor's papers, a dirty ten-bob note and a photograph of a naked woman in it. That's all...'

'Well?'

'Well? Well wot? Where are his clothes and his kit-bag? Isabel says she hasn't got them. The police say they've searched for them and can't find them.'

'Perhaps he left them on his ship when he went off on the spree at which he was arrested.'

'He did not. He had his bag with him at the time of the spree that you call it and when he was gaoled, it was put in the prison cloakroom, or whatever they call it, and would be handed out again when he was released. Are you aware that I was the only one who visited him in gaol?'

'No.'

'There you are, you see. You don't know everything in the police, do you? I'm an important witness in this affair. I ought to have been interviewed.'

'I'm very sorry, Mr. Handy. We have still a lot of people to interrogate and your name is among them...'

'It's taken you long enough. When will I be seeing you?'

'Tomorrow? Unless you've something more you wish to tell me now.'

'Over the 'phone? Not likely. I've spent all my small change as it is. I'm in a public call-box. The police ought to reimburse me for this expense.'

'I'll see you get it...'

'One and six. I'll be out on my milk round till noon. Inspector Knell knows where the farm is...'

Judging from the noise at the other end, the telephone was about to register another sixpence, so Littlejohn bade Mr. Handy a hasty good night and went to join his friends. He told them about the information Sydney Handy had given him. Knell was surprised to hear that Handy had visited his brother-in-law in gaol.

'Interfering in his usual pompous way. I'll bet Joss Varran was glad to be rid of him when he left. There's no account of this visit on the records. We'd better ask Syd what it was all about when we see him tomorrow.'

The Archdeacon then insisted that Knell return home and have a good night's sleep.

'You've had a heavy day today, and tomorrow isn't likely to be less strenuous.'

The old grandfather clock in the hall struck eleven as they saw him off from the vicarage door. The village was asleep and all the lights were out. Somewhere, far away, a dog was barking, but until Knell started his car, there wasn't another sound outside. There had been a long drought and the river was low and flowed silently under the bridge.

Maggie Keggin had left a tray for them, with cups and a tin of cocoa on the kitchen table, and they made themselves a drink apiece. Then, after Littlejohn had rung up his wife in Hampstead and they had exchanged the news of the day, he and the Archdeacon went to their beds. Littlejohn was asleep before midnight.

Knell, busily occupied by routine, called at Grenaby for Littlejohn and the Archdeacon late the following morning and they arrived at Sydney Handy's farm at Narradale just after noon. This was reached by a turning from the main Ramsey Road at a spot called Ginger Hall, whence the secondary road rose through splendid country, wooded in parts, with magnificent views of the surrounding landscape. Handy's farm, Ballablock, lay hidden in the hills, a rather ramshackle holding with a stone farmhouse which bore the year 1807 over the door and looked as if it hadn't had much attention since.

Sydney was in the yard, noisily throwing milk churns about and met them with reproach. His eye was still discoloured and he moved about stiffly as though he'd got rheumatism.

'You're late. Here was I rushing round with milk on me round to be here in time. I said I'd be back at noon...'

Knell apologised without much sincerity.

'We're busy, too, you know, Mr. Handy.'

'You'd better come inside. I'm on my own. The wife's gone to see her sister about the funeral. I needn't tell you that the Varrans are hopeless where initiative's concerned. They're always on the look-out for somebody else to do the work for them...'

Judging from the tumbledown buildings, the scraggy hens picking in the farmyard and the gaunt sheep and cattle struggling for food on the surrounding hillsides, Mr. Handy was afflicted by the same complaint, but Knell didn't care to argue with him. He knew Syd's rather pathetic history already. For some reason, known only to herself, Rose Varran had joined the W.A.A.F. during the war and, on her travels had met and married Syd, who came from Stockport on the mainland. Handy hadn't known the first thing about farming, but was sure his initiative would see him through. He had always been an ambitious optimist. In his dreams he saw farms, flocks of prize-winning sheep and pedigree herds of cattle, wallets bulging with banknotes, and cabinets showing off silver plate. All of it his. And here he was...

'Come in...'

Mr. Handy led the way to a small sitting-room, so full of shabby furniture that they could hardly get in it. Much of this Mr. Handy had inherited from his mother, who had once kept a second-hand furniture shop and had come to live with them after their marriage. She had insisted on bringing most of her belongings with her, in case they didn't get on well together and she had to set up house on her own again. She had died the previous year and Syd, full of 'initiative', had insisted on keeping his inheritance intact, as he was sure it would 'go up'. The other rooms of the farmhouse were in a similar confused jam and in the main bedroom there were four beds, two of which Syd said were antiques and would increase in value with the keeping.

Mr. Handy indicated chairs set round a table, the top of which had warped with the damp, and they all sat down, Mr. Handy at the head like the chairman at a board meeting.

'With one thing and another, there's quite a lot to be said, so we'd better get busy,' said Sydney Handy. 'You all know the verdict at the inquest will be murder. Why can't we bury 'im? It's not good enough holding things up like this.'

'This is a matter for the coroner, Mr. Handy. The real reason for our visit here is because you told us that you'd visited your brother-in-law in prison. What made you do that?'

Mr. Handy looked at Knell angrily.

'I might have expected a comment like that from you. Can't a man have pity, have bowels of compassion for somebody without his motives being questioned? I visited Joss Varran because there was nobody else to visit him. Can you imagine turning Isabel loose in London? She's never been off the Island. Somebody had to go. It was only decent...'

'Did you go to gaol on business, Handy?'

The Archdeacon asked the question this time and Mr. Handy perhaps thought he'd better tell the truth to one of the cloth.

'There were bills to pay, the upkeep of the house, rates etcetera. Isabel couldn't afford it and I certainly wasn't going to foot Joss Varran's bills, knowing the type he was...'

He made little pecking jerks with his beaky nose, punctuating all he said. Otherwise, his face was quite expressionless, like a stupid mask.

'But it would cost you far more in fares to make the trip than all the expenses of running Close Dhoo put together. Surely, you had some other reason.'

Littlejohn intervened and Handy's attitude changed at once. Beads of sweat appeared on his upper lip. The magic of Scotland Yard must have scared him.

'Tell us from the beginning what happened, Mr. Handy.'

'Nothing much. That's the funny part of it.'

'Start at the beginning. What made you wish to visit your brother-in-law? It wasn't charity. It was something more vital and compulsive to you, wasn't it?'

'He wrote to Isabel and asked her to come. He wanted specially to see her. And she was afraid to go. She'd written to him regularly and she said she'd even suggested herself that she might go to see him. He'd never replied. Then came this letter asking her to go. She got scared. So I said I'd go for her.'

'She paid expenses?'

'I was going on her account. You can't reproach me with that. I'm not rich and besides, I left the farm and my work for two days...'

'What happened when you saw Joss?'

'Nothing.'

'You talked, I suppose. What did you talk about?'

'I thought he'd sent for Isabel to talk over family matters or such like. Or else, he wanted something and was after money. Instead, if he hadn't been such a tough fellow, with no feelings at all, I'd have said he was homesick. He asked about Isabel and how she was going on. I said she was all right and managing nicely and that she hadn't come herself because she was scared, never having been off the Island before.'

'What else?'

'He asked about the house, and was it all right. Funny that. From him that was hardly ever at home and never interested in the state of the place or even if Isabel had money enough to keep it going. He even asked about the land, too. Said he'd seen in the paper that they were testing in various parts of the Island for oil. Had anybody been digging round Close Dhoo? Because if they had, we'd better let him know as he'd want to be in at any business arising. I told him there was no fear of that. Nobody had been round there digging and weren't likely to. I thought that was funny, but he seemed to want to talk about the Island. He even asked about the Candells, who he'd never spoken to for years, and if Quantrell was still about the place and the Duffys. It went on like that till the time was up. In the end I asked him if he wanted to tell me or Isabel something particular or wanted us to do anything for him. He said No. Just like that. No, Syd, thanks and good-bye.'

'And that was all?'

'The lot. What do you make of it?'

'Perhaps he was lonely and wanted to see somebody from home.'

'What? Joss? Not him.'

'When was this, Mr. Handy?'

'Last autumn. He said I was the only visitor he'd had since he was put inside.'

'And that's all?'

'Yes. And before you go, I ask you again, what happened to Joss's belongings? The police say they haven't seen them. He must have had his kit-bag with him when he left the prison. Where is it now? His money and some clothes and his razor and the like must have been in it. He'd only ten shillings in his wallet. A man doesn't travel that distance on a dirty ten-bob note. He must have had more in his kit-bag and if you ask me somebody's pinched it.'

They thanked him and left him. He seemed bewildered by it all now and the last they saw of him he was wandering about the yard as though he didn't quite know where he was.

They decided to call at the manor again and have a further talk with Duffy and Quantrell. On the way, they met Kincaid in his van. He signalled to them and pulled up.

He saluted Littlejohn smartly and then turned his attentions to Knell.

'I was wanting to see you, sir. Earlier this morning I had E. D. Cojeen at my place. He said he'd just passed by Close Dhoo and called to express his condolences, as he called them, to Isabel. She asked him to give me a message if he was coming my way. It was that last night, she went into the shed at the back of the house to get some paraffin for the fire and she found some of Joss's clothes in a bundle in one corner. There was his razor among them and nearly fifty pounds in money. I'm just on my way to Close Dhoo now to investigate. Cojeen, when I asked him, said Joss's kit-bag wasn't with the rest. He'd asked Isabel, because that's the sort of thing a sailor usually has in his bag...'

'We'll come with you, Kincaid,' said Knell, and they all went off together.

Chapter IX
The 'Mary Peters'

Isabel Varran was at home, busily occupied in turning out the house. Now that Joss was dead the property was her own, for Joss, in an unexpected gesture, had long ago made a will and left to her all that he had. She was turning over a new leaf and asserting an unusual independence. Her sister, Mrs. Handy, declaring that blood was thicker than water in spite of her husband's protests, had taken Isabel's side. Mr. Handy had denounced the will as unjust and threatened to contest it, a forlorn hope, but characteristic of his 'initiative' which, at every crisis in his life had let him down.

Rose had, Isabel told her visitors, gone to Ramsey in the van and there proposed to make the funeral arrangements and find a lawyer to deal with the will. This act of charity had been undertaken before Isabel had found the money in the outhouse and when the Handys had thought that only the house at Close Dhoo was covered by the will. What would happen when they discovered that there was now cash as well was anybody's guess.

The bundle of clothes, money and personal effects found by Isabel in the woodshed was lying on the table when Knell and his friends entered the house. Isabel told them how she had found it. It seemed to indicate that Joss Varran had arrived home whilst Isabel was asleep by the fire, but before entering he had dealt with the matter foremost in his mind, the digging up of the treasure, or whatever it was, from its hiding place in the bog. And probably, to make available something in which to carry it, he had emptied his kit-bag in the outhouse, where he may have been finding a spade. Whoever had killed Joss had carried off the bag and its precious contents.

Isabel who seemed to regard the police as her friends, hospitably provided them with tea and soda cakes again as Knell examined the property abandoned by her brother. She seemed quite bewildered by it.

'Why should he throw his things and all that money in the shed, instead of bringing it in the house?'

'He must have been in a hurry to unearth and take away whatever was hidden in the Shaking Field. And he probably didn't wish you to know and ask questions about it. Have you any idea what it might have been?'

'No. I'm as puzzled as you are.'

'Did Joss come home on his last trip in the *Mary Peters* to Ramsey before he went to gaol?' asked Littlejohn.

'Yes. I remember it. He arrived early in the morning before I'd got up. It was dark.'

'Had he been drinking?'

'Not as much as usual. He came earlier than he'd been in the habit of doing. He was in a good temper for once.'

'Did he seem excited about anything?'

'Funny you should ask that. He seemed very pleased with himself.'

'Did he say why?'

'He said, after I'd quizzed him a bit, that he'd another job in mind, with better pay and when I asked where it was, he said over in England. I didn't push him to tell me more. I'd heard the same story before.'

'Do you remember the date?'

'Yes, I do. It was early on March 24th. I'd had a rates demand which was due on the 30th and he usually paid it. I remember the date exactly because it was just a week before the final date for payment. I told him so. He said he'd give me the money before he left for his ship, but he didn't. He was like that. He never said "Good-bye" or "Take care". Just up and away.'

'He had his kit-bag with him on that occasion?'

'Yes. He always had it with him when he came home from sea. I used to wash the soiled clothes he brought home in it. I don't know why he didn't have it when he came home from prison.'

'But he did have it when he arrived, apparently. And he emptied it in the shed to make room in it for carrying whatever he dug out of the bog.'

Isabel looked worried.

'What was it?'

'I don't know. Probably money.'

'But he never had much money…'

'Do you remember who brought Joss home from Ramsey just before he went off and got gaoled?'

'Yes, I do. He came in a taxi. I remember it well. I saw the taxi. It came right to the door. When I complained about the expense, Joss brushed it aside. He actually said he'd soon have a car of his own, although where he was going to get the money from I don't know. He only stayed for less than an hour, and he kept the taxi waiting. He told me to shut up when I asked him why he was in such a hurry.'

'Before that occasion, how did Joss usually get home when his boat docked in Ramsey after the last bus had gone?'

'It isn't hard to get a lift from Ramsey as far as Ballaugh. After that, if you aren't lucky, you've to walk from Ballaugh the rest of the way.'

There was a pause. The wind was getting up again. It hardly ceased there at that time of year. Now and then a gust brought a puff of aromatic smoke down the chimney into the room. Outside, the willow and bog myrtle bushes on the roadsides shook in all directions.

'Do you know the Duffys from the manor house, Miss Varran?'

'She sometimes passes here on her horse, but we've never spoken.'

She looked straight at Littlejohn wondering what it was all about.

'Did Joss know them?'

'He might have done, but he never told me. Never even mentioned them. Why, sir?'

'We've been told that on the night he died he got a lift from Ramsey in an old car which might have been the one belonging to the Duffys. That seemed to indicate they knew one another if it was their car.'

'I wouldn't know. He never said anything before about them. Are you sure it was the Duffys?'

'Not absolutely. But there are only three vintage cars – old cars, you know – of the kind described to us as giving Joss a lift, on the Island. One is quite out of commission, the other is away on a rally in England. That leaves only the Duffys' car. And the Duffys say they weren't out in it that night. So, there we are.'

'Who told you that Joss was seen in the old car?'

'Mr. Cojeen ... '

Isabel threw her hands up and shrieked.

'*Mister* Cojeen, was it? Cojeen the Rags? He'd tell you anything. They used to call him Cojeen the Liar, until he got to know about it and threatened to take it to court.'

'Why should he lie to the police?'

'Just to seem clever.'

There seemed no point in further questioning and discussion. It was obvious that E. D. Cojeen wasn't popular with Isabel Varran, to say the least of it. Knell would have to find out his reputation from someone less prejudiced. This was soon forthcoming. After they had thanked Isabel and said good-bye and the door was closed again, Kincaid saved them any further trouble.

'I wouldn't put too much on what Isabel Varran says about E. D. Cojeen, sir. Some years ago, E. D. took a bit of a fancy to Isabel and got to calling at Close Dhoo pretty regular. One day Joss came home unexpected and found him with his feet under the table enjoying a meal. Joss had the drink in him and hit E. D. on the nose and chucked him out of the house. That was the end of that. And that, I reckon, is why Isabel is trying to cast doubt on E. D.'s testimony. He's harmless enough.'

Littlejohn changed the subject.

'When is the *Mary Peters* due in Ramsey next, Kincaid?'

'She's tied up there now. She's due off on the night tide.'

'We'd better get along to Ramsey then. We don't wish to wait until she turns up there again several days from now.'

After a hasty lunch at the local hotel again, they made for Ramsey. It had rained there during the night and the town and sea front had a pleasant well-washed appearance and the sky was clear and the air invigorating. There was a slight breeze and the calm water of the port lapped gently against the stone quays. Here and there, idlers had gathered, talking in small groups.

The *Mary Peters* was tied up in the river, loading containers. She was trim and well-kept. A smell of hot oil hung around her. Nearby a Norwegian boat was unloading timber. Piles of damp planks standing on the quay ready for loading on lorries gave off a fragrant smell. Chains and winches rattled. Little pleasure boats, tied up here and there, added colour to the scene. A brewers' dray was drawn up nearby and two brawny men were discharging metal barrels of beer.

Knell drove to the narrow gangway which connected the *Mary Peters* with the quay. Overhead, a crane was hoisting the cargo aboard. A man leaning over the rail smoking a pipe and spitting in the water called to them before they even had time to enquire for the captain.

'Wantin' somethin'?'

'Is Captain Buckle aboard?'

'In his cabin eatin' his dinner.'

'Tell him we want to see him, please. We're from the police.'

The man gave them a hard look and made off in the direction of the bridge. Some deck-hands stopped work and waited expectantly. The knots of idlers on the quay suddenly grew animated. It was as though a soundless message had passed from group to group and they all began to move nearer to the ship to obtain ringside seats for what they were sure was going to be a dramatic encounter. They were disappointed. The sailor reappeared.

'Come aboard. He's in his cabin. This way...'

They followed him to the small, neat cabin under the bridge. The sailor ushered them in without another word and disappeared. Outside the crane was whining and men were shouting.

The captain was eating steak puddings and potatoes piled on a large thick plate on a mahogany table covered with a square of oil-cloth. He rose to greet them. He was a square-set fair man with a big belly and close-cropped hair. He knew Knell.

'Hello, Mr. Knell. To what do we owe this pleasure?'

He sucked his teeth and eyed the Archdeacon suspiciously, puzzled by his presence there. Knell introduced his friends and told Buckle right away why they had called on him.

'Sit down, if you can find room.'

There was only another chair besides that the captain was occupying, but opposite where he was sitting was an alcove containing a long seat like a shelf. The three new-comers seated themselves side by side on it, like patients in a doctor's waiting-room.

'Mind if I get on with my dinner? There's a lot to be done before we leave on the evening tide.'

He resumed his enjoyment of his steak puddings, although by now they had gone cold and greasy-looking. He didn't seem to mind and talked as he ate.

'Joss Varran? I heard about him. He was murdered near his home, wasn't he?'

He took a good drink from a large glass of stout at his elbow and wiped his mouth on the back of his hand.

'I can't see that I'll be much help to you about that. I haven't seen Varran since he left the *Mary Peters* in London and landed himself in gaol. Nice mess he made of things for me, getting himself and two more of my crew remanded in custody. I'd to take on two fresh hands. He pleaded guilty to the charge of drunken violence, or something of the kind, so I wasn't needed in court. I never saw him again alive.'

'It's about what happened before he made his last trip to London that we're concerned now. What date would that be?'

'A year last March...'

He turned and took a dog-eared notebook from a drawer in a chest behind him. Licking his forefinger he slowly turned over the pages.

'Here we are. March 28th.'

'You run a regular schedule of services?'

'We do. Twice weekly each way, with occasional runs to London as circumstances arise.'

The captain, having finished his main meal and disposed of with apparent relish a piece of revolting apple tart, took out a short pipe and lit the remains of his last smoke.

'How long had Varran been with you?'

'About two years before they gaoled him. He was with us almost from the beginning of these Preston-Ramsey runs. We only started them about four years ago, mainly container traffic.'

'What did he do before that?'

'A casual deck-hand. He was a restless sort of chap. Never in one job for long. He seemed more settled after I took him on. You see, it gave him a chance of getting home more frequently. Not that he was what I'd call a home-bird, but he seemed attached to Ramsey and its locality.'

'Could you give us some clearer details of Varran's movements immediately prior to his imprisonment?'

Captain Buckle consulted his grubby little book again and Knell took down the details he patiently read out from it.

March	23rd	Preston-Ramsey. 22.00
		Varran went ashore at Ramsey, with permission.
	24th	Varran aboard again, 7.0 a.m.
	25th	Ramsey-Preston 3.0 a.m.
	26th	Preston-London 11.00 a.m.
	28th	London, 18.00

'I've got fuller details in the log...'

'Leave them for the time being. We'll ask you later if we need them,' said Littlejohn. 'Varran was with two of his shipmates when he was arrested?'

'Yes. The other two were remanded, but got off with fines. It was Varran who was violent. The other two were charged with being drunk and disorderly.'

'Who were they?'

'Sam Carran and Charlie Bott.'

'Still members of your crew?'

'Bott is. He's a good man. No reason for holding his escapade against him. Sailors like their little fling ashore. Sam Carran got a job on Liverpool docks. He said he was tired of the sea, but I think his wife had a finger in the change.'

'Is Bott around?'

'He's probably on deck.'

'May we have him in?'

Captain Buckle wobbled to the door and put his head out of the cabin.

'Bott! Bott!'

There was a lot of incoherent shouting outside as Buckle's voice rang round the quayside. Several dogs started to bark.

A little slip of a man in old trousers and a seaman's jersey put his head round the door. He squinted at the assembled party and looked ready to run away again.

'Come in, Bott.'

'Yes, sir.'

'The police want a word with you, Bott.'

Bott had been drunk the night before and wondered if he'd been disorderly again, although he couldn't remember it. He fixed his eyes anxiously on the Archdeacon, as though he might have broken the law of God as well as men.

'Well, come in. They're not after you, although judging from the looks of you, you might have been up to something.'

'I haven't done a thing, Captain. I swear...'

'Shut up and listen. They want to see you about Varran.'

'I had nothing to do with it. I didn't even know he was out.'

'Will you be quiet and answer their questions. Nobody said you murdered Varran. It's about the brawl you joined in on the London docks.'

'Tell us exactly what happened, Bott. Who started it all?' said Littlejohn.

'It was Varran, sir. He'd never been like that before. The funny thing was he'd not had all that much to drink. I've seen him nice and peaceable on far more than he had that night. If he'd wanted to get himself put inside, he couldn't have been worse. He deliberately provoked a Welshman who was a friendly chap, just taking his drink quietly. He kept saying that one Manxman was as good as three Welsh. Over and over again. In the end the man hit him. I'd have done the same myself. And that started it. They went outside to settle it and on the way, Varran picked up an empty bottle and smashed it so that he had the jagged neck in his hand. Well... Sam Carran and me got hold of Varran and tried to stop him. There was a mix-up, others joining in, and the police were there in no time. As I said, if Varran had wanted to get himself a stretch in gaol, he couldn't have done more. The rest of us got fines, but the broken bottle and Joss's previous record for drunkenness went against him. You see, he went for the police with the bottle, too. Lucky they got him before he did some real damage, although there was blood about.'

'Had you and Varran been shipmates long?'

'Two years about.'

'Had he been behaving badly or queerly before the affair at London docks?'

'He'd been jumpy. As a matter of fact, him and Carran, who was a good shipmate of Varran's, had had a row only a few days before.'

'What about?'

'Something and nothing. Carran said Varran was suggestin' that he was a thief. It all blew over.'

'Why was Carran a thief, Bott?'

'He wasn't. Never a man more honest.'

'What was all the fuss about, then?'

Bott was chewing what might have been tobacco. He paused in his chewing, as he tried to remember exactly what, had happened. Then, he began again with a curious twisting thrust of his jaw.

'It's a long time since and I'm trying to remember how it all started. Varran was a bit late aboard. We were due to sail at ten, I seem to recollect, and he was only just in time. He arrived, carrying a white parcel, like a pillow-slip, full of something...'

'Was he drunk?'

'No. Which was unusual. He was always at least half drunk when he'd been long ashore. He'd had a drink, I know, but that was all. I remember he took a good swig of rum that he kept in a bottle in his locker, when he arrived. Then he tucked the parcel in his bunk under the blankets. He wasn't as a rule so careful about his kit. Matter of fact, he always left his things lying about. That's what Carran remarked about. He asked him what was so precious that he needed to tuck it away in bed. Joking like. Varran flared up and they'd a real row.'

'And Varran carefully looked after his parcel until he left the ship...?'

'That's right. He was so busy looking after his parcel, that he forgot to take his kit-bag with him and we had to shout him back to remind him.'

'Did he seem excited?'

'When he came aboard he'd been running, I think. He was out of breath and red in the face. When he'd gone, Carran and me said we thought he'd been with some woman and stayed a bit over his time.'

'Can you describe the parcel? Have you any idea what was in it?'

'Your guess is as good as mine. We hardly saw it. He had it with him in his bunk.'

'Wasn't he on watch during the journey?'

'No. He said he had pains in his stomach and he asked me to take his watch for him. Which I did, after reporting to the mate. I thought Varran had a nerve to ask either of us to stand-in for him after the way he'd behaved to us. He said he was sorry.'

'And that was all?'

'Yes. A queer do, but then Varran was a queer chap. We was used to him and what's the use of holding a grudge against a shipmate? It only makes things awkward.'

Bott stood there, holding himself up against the door-post and glancing from one to another of the party with shifty eyes. He was still puzzled by the Archdeacon's presence there.

'Now, about your escapade in London again, Bott. Did you get the impression that Varran deliberately provoked the row and the fight?'

'Me and Carran couldn't understand it at all. There was no sense in it. You'd have thought he was deliberately trying to land himself in gaol. A bit of a scrap is one thing when you've got the drink in you. But a broken bottle and then assaulting the police...He was asking for it. And he got it. Varran himself was a bit put out at the sentence they gave him, but it seems there'd been a lot of rough stuff going on at the docks at the time and the magistrates said they were determined to stamp it out. The police threw the book at Varran, too.'

'What reason could Varran have had for wanting to be put in gaol?'

'Don't ask me, sir. I said Varran was a queer bloke. One minute all smiles, the next in a hell of a temper.'

'That will be all then, Bott. Thanks for your help.'

The captain was anxious to see him back at work.

'All right, then, Bott. You can go.'

The man showed a clean pair of heels, obviously wanting to join his mates and circulate his tale.

For the time being there seemed little else to be gained by discussion with Captain Buckle. He repeated his opinion of Varran, that, as a seaman, he worked hard, but was taciturn and impulsive, resented authority somewhat and was restless and unsettled.

'Hardly what you'd call a good testimonial, Captain,' remarked the Archdeacon.

Captain Buckle shrugged his shoulders.

'They can be as temperamental as they like, sir, provided they work during working hours and keep the ship peaceful and don't upset the crew. Also, they've to obey orders. That's all. If they're unsettled, they can't do anything about it once we're on the way and if they sign-off when we get to port, there's always somebody else. I'd never any trouble with Varran.'

They thanked him and left him still brooding in his cabin and made for Grenaby. Knell was anxious to get back to headquarters to deal with reports and routine, but they all agreed that they had better sort out the information they had gathered and Maggie Keggin arrived with tea to refresh them.

'What do you think, sir?'

Knell asked Littlejohn as though he thought that the Chief Superintendent had already arrived at a conclusion.

'We seem to have a clearer picture of Varran and his comings and goings before he landed in gaol. On March 23rd, he arrived aboard the *Mary Peters* in a hurry, flushed and panting from haste. He carried a bundle with him which he didn't wish his shipmates to see or know anything about. He quarrelled with Carran for merely making a jocular enquiry about it. We can assume that he pretended to be unwell when he was due to go on watch simply to be able to remain with his parcel and protect it. It must have been something valuable and, probably, suspicious or illegal. He paid a short visit to Close Dhoo and then was off very early to join his ship. Isabel says he arrived by taxi. You'd better try to find the taxi driver who took him there and back.'

'Meanwhile, having hidden his bundle in his father's hiding place in the bog,' added Knell, after making a note about the taxi.

'Exactly. Suppose Varran had committed a crime, say a robbery, and the parcel held the loot. And until the heat was off, he decided to hide it. That theory explains quite a lot of what happened. Now, let's assume he had an accomplice or more than one in the crime and he'd either made off with the plunder himself or else they'd left him to dispose of it until it was safe to get rid of it and share the spoils. What happened after he'd hidden his precious bundle?'

Knell took the question literally and answered it.

'He was back aboard early next morning. He was there by seven o'clock. Then back to Preston and on to London, where he got himself gaoled.'

'According to Bott, Varran almost invited the police to put him in gaol. Why?'

The Archdeacon who had been following the account with deep interest took a turn.

'It suggests to me that Varran had decided to elude his accomplices and keep the loot himself. He made for the ship, which was almost ready for off. Presumably, someone followed him, but was unable to get at him aboard. Varran knew that they could only follow him by boat or plane early next day. So, he got aboard the *Mary Peters* again, where he was safe. Thence to Preston, with his friends still after him. He presumably kept aboard until the ship sailed for London. There matters changed. He couldn't skulk aboard for ever if he found a reception committee of his accomplices waiting there for him. So, he left the ship with his shipmates. There he must have seen his pursuers. What could he do about it?'

Knell gave the Archdeacon an astonished look.

'You mean to suggest he decided to get himself run-in by the police as the best way out?'

'Certainly. His accomplices were desperate men, Knell. Remember they eventually murdered Joss Varran. He couldn't tell his shipmates that he'd committed a crime nor depend on them to join in a rough-house if his pursuers attacked him. Bott told us he seemed anxious to provoke a brawl and even to involve himself in an assault on the police. Varran was completely independent. No wife and family. Only a sister he didn't care a hoot about. Once in gaol he would be safe, although, it seems, he didn't expect to be there as long as that. But he overdid it and got a long stretch. He was quite secure from his brothers in crime and,

if my information is correct, good food and very modern
conveniences now go with prison punishment. The only
snag was that the loot was safely hidden so far away and
if his partners were tenaciously awaiting him outside, he'd
have to run the gauntlet again. Which he did and was killed
for his pains. We've two problems before we can proceed
with certainty. Who were his accomplices and what was in
Varran's precious bag which he protected so fiercely?'

Littlejohn lit his pipe and rose.

'Mind if I use the telephone? We can, at least, find out if
anything exciting in the way of crime occurred in Preston
on the night Joss Varran arrived aboard the *Mary Peters* with
what Bott called his pillow-slip. Superintendent Peregrine,
of the County Police, and I were on the beat together in
Manchester when we were young...'

He was not long away and returned smiling.

'Got it! They didn't even need to turn up the records.
On the date in question three men robbed the Preston
Branch of Housmans Bank. They were disturbed, but all
three escaped. One of them, who was holding the bag, carried it off with him. It was half-full and contained twenty-
five thousand pounds in soiled notes. What a marvellous
getaway! A ship ready waiting for off and the man with the
bag was one of the crew. It must have been Joss Varran.'

CHAPTER X
DISASTER AT BALLABLOCK

The following morning, a sheaf of reports arrived at Douglas headquarters concerning a number of characters connected with the Close Dhoo crime.

The photographs of the Duffys and Quantrell at the veteran car rally had been circulated and information had come in from Preston and Liverpool.

The Duffys were known in Ribchester, a suburb of Preston, whence they had removed to the Isle of Man, presumably in search of cheaper taxation. There had been some doubt about the relationship of the pair of them, but they appeared to have led a quiet life in a nice house in the village. They had, according to local information, arrived in Ribchester from London, where the Colonel had said he had been in the wine trade. Sarah Duffy posed as his daughter, although some of their neighbours thought differently. There was no record at all at Preston about Quantrell.

Superintendent Peregrine, of Preston, was a member of the same club as Williams, the manager of Housmans Bank, who had been the Duffys' next-door neighbour when they were in Ribchester and he had asked Williams about the Colonel. Williams had reported Duffy to be a good neighbour, a quiet sort, no bother at all. Now and then, Williams and Duffy had a drink together. 'As a matter of fact,' Williams had remarked, 'I called on them when I was stay-ing on holiday on the Isle of Man a year ago last March. Nice place they have there, but a bit too big for them. It's getting neglected.' Peregrine had added a final note concerning his informant. 'A very decent fellow and reliable. Manager of Housmans Bank, in Preston. Quite a large business.'

Littlejohn got in touch with Peregrine over the tele-phone right away, thanked him for his help and asked a question.

'Did Duffy and Williams talk banking whilst Williams was visiting him?'

'I can't be sure, but I could find out definitely. Williams talks banking most of his time. He's banking mad. He'd be sure to get on his favourite hobby-horse, especially as Housmans were extending their premises at the time and Williams was excited about it. They were having their old strong-room enlarged and modernised and the main big door hadn't arrived up to schedule. As the old door had been dismantled, the cash and safe custody was housed in a number of first-class small safes temporarily. It made the robbery so much easier, as there was no strong-room door to open. Just the safes. There were, of course, a clerk and a watchman there on guard and the police called regularly. The robbers arrived just after one of our men had left, and they tied up the two men on watch. Judging from the knots, the man who trussed them up had been a sailor...'

'You've no idea who did the job?'

'Not a thing.'

'Did you get a description of the men?'

'Not even that. I suppose they wore the usual stockings over their faces, but they didn't need them. They weren't violent. Simply chloroformed the guards before they were even aware of what was going on.'

'They were disturbed, weren't they, and got away with only part of the loot?'

'Yes. Four of the safes held cash. They opened the one controlled by the chief cashier and got away with about twenty-five thousand pounds. The deputy manager happened to make a surprise call on his way home from a dinner and disturbed and scared them off. They got away in the dark and apparently broke up, one of them carrying the spoils. The deputy or the chloroformed men didn't get a good look at any of them. All the deputy could say was that one of them was big and burly, one was fairly tall and well wrapped up, and the other was medium height, strongly built and was a good runner.'

'Not a very easy case ... '

'No. It's still unsolved. We haven't got a clue.'

'Well, here might be a line worth pursuing. Ask Williams if he told Duffy all about the plans for the new building and, in particular, if he gave him any details about the new strong-room.'

'I'll do that and let you know. Surely Duffy wasn't part of the gang who did it? He was very respectable when he lived in these parts.'

The next report, this time from Scotland Yard, proved that Peregrine had been mistaken.

The Duffy pair had been recognised from the photographs. They had both Duffy and his 'daughter' on the files. Her name was Sarah Heron, but she called herself Duffy for convenience. Confidence tricksters, frequently in the best circles, and they had both been in gaol. Bouncing cheques, share pushing, phoney antiques, long-term frauds ... the lot. They had disappeared from London after their last effort, a bogus charity, for which they had both served time. A very plausible couple, especially the woman, who possessed good looks and charm as well as ingenuity and she seemed quite well-bred.

It appeared to Littlejohn that the Duffys had retired to an isolated spot on the Isle of Man with their ill-gotten gains, but had been unable to resist the Preston bank affair after Williams had talked so enthusiastically about it. It must have, in the beginning, looked very easy and promising, only to finish with Varran scooping the lot and then, when they were after him for their shares, he'd sought a safe refuge for the time being – gaol. No wonder Duffy was drinking and going to seed and Sarah bitter and savage.

Littlejohn was with Knell in his office after perusing the reports.

The Liverpool report on Quantrell was short but to the point. Quantrell had seven years ago been given a sentence of four years for robbing a firm of wine merchants in Bootle. That was the only really serious charge against him and after serving time, Quantrell had subsided and disappeared, either to turn over a new leaf or else to pursue his criminal designs elsewhere. He had, with two others, broken in the warehouse and they had opened and rifled the safe, which contained the wages for the next day, and carried off a considerable quantity of spirits. The criminals had been traced through their untimely consumption and efforts to dispose of the latter. In the course of the case it had come to light that Quantrell had opened the safe. He came of a very decent family and his father had once been a highly esteemed workman in a firm of safe makers, on the strength of which, when he retired to his native land and became a blacksmith, his son had followed in his footsteps until he had served his full apprenticeship. Young Quantrell had

lost his job on personal grounds. He had been decidedly
left-wing in his politics and had fomented a strike.

'So there we seem to have one of the Preston gang,' said
Littlejohn. 'With an operator like Quantrell loose in society,
there's no telling how many other unsolved safe-breaking
crimes he's been involved in. We'd better see Quantrell right
away. That makes two of the gang. Quantrell and Varran.
Who's number three? The Colonel? Or even Sarah Duffy?'

There was another contribution from Scotland Yard.
They had made enquiries about Varran's visitors during his
spell in gaol and telephoned the results to Knell.

There had been only two of them. Varran had made it
plain from the start that he didn't wish to see anybody from
outside. On May 14th, just after his imprisonment, a woman
had called and asked for him. She had given the name of
Mildred Watson and the prison officials had assumed she
was Varran's girl. He had refused to see her. The officer
who had interviewed her remembered what she had looked
like. He had thought her what he described as a cut above
Varran and, on being shown the newspaper photograph of
Sarah Duffy, had said he thought it was she and if it wasn't
it was someone very like her.

The only other visitor had been Sydney Handy, Varran's
brother-in-law, who arrived on September 1st of the same
year. Varran had sent for him, saying that he wished to see
him on a family matter.

Scotland Yard added a note that they were occupied
in finding the whereabouts of Varran's cell mates, John
(Cracker Jack) Jukes and Cliff Larkin. On his release,
Jukes had gone to Monte Carlo with his wife, presumably
with the help of some hidden loot. During his imprisonment, he had evolved a system which he was sure would
break the bank. Was it necessary for someone to pursue

him to the Riviera and question him? Larkin was living in Tasman Road, Poplar, and would be interviewed. Report to follow.

And just as Littlejohn and Knell were about to leave for Close Dhoo, Peregrine telephoned from Preston to say that he had spoken to Williams, the bank manager, who said quite plainly that he had told Duffy of his building and removal problems connected with the new bank premises and he'd also complained about the current habit of contractors in exceeding the time of completion. He remembered lamenting that even the once meticulous safe makers had let him down and how he was having a lot of trouble and expense in consequence.

'I asked him if he discussed details of arrangements to tide him over until the strong-room was finally ready. He said Duffy seemed very interested in it all and asked a lot of questions.'

'And he wasn't suspicious?'

'No. He said Duffy actually commented that it all reminded him of some of the crime stories on television. Williams said Duffy was the last man he'd expect to commit such a crime and that he didn't believe for a moment that he'd had anything to do with it at all.'

It was a fine morning and the drive over the hills and along the mountain road to Ramsey and then on through the straight flat lands with their great leafy trees was indeed pleasant. Knell kept interrupting their professional conversation to point out local beauty spots and places of interest in a proud, wondering manner as though he were seeing the beauty of his native land for the first time. He even commented favourably about the tumbledown Close Dhoo, from the chimney of which the white wood smoke was rising straight into the clear sky.

'It reminds me of the old days and the old folk. Decent people they were, even though they were poor. Different from this lot with their robbing banks and murdering one another and chasing one another all over the place as if the devil were after them...'

They met the Archdeacon at Ballaugh. He had remained at Grenaby to finish his next Sunday's sermon and promised to join them later. One of his parishioners had driven him there.

When they reached Close Dhoo washing was hanging on the line in the garden and Isabel Varran was feverishly gathering it in lest the visitors should see and identify her underwear. She greeted them in her usual fashion. She welcomed the Archdeacon with special cordiality.

'I'll make some tea.'

They told her they hadn't time to stay, but she ignored the information and spread out her best tea-set again and produced cake and drinks before she would listen to them.

'We called to ask why Mr. Handy went to London to see him not long after Joss had been put in gaol.'

'I don't really know, Mr. Knell. He wrote to Sydney and said he wanted to see him on family business. He said in his note to Syd that nobody else must come and that me and Rose would get lost in London and upset with the prison and him inside it. I couldn't get a proper tale out of Syd. He said it was something and nothing when he got to the prison and he thought that Joss was feeling a bit homesick and wanted to see somebody from the family... Syd got properly annoyed when Rose and me tried to get more out of him. So we left him alone. He said Joss was all right and looking forward to getting home, although he was decently treated in prison.'

She thanked Knell for his kindness to her at the inquest.

'The funeral is tomorrow...'

She was completely different from the woman they had met for the first time a few days ago. Her plaintive manner and shyness seemed to have gone under the influence of her new independence and the end of the worry caused by her brother and his unruly habits.

'Have you seen Mr. Handy lately?'

'No. He hasn't been near. Rose has done most of the arrangements. He says he's too busy on the farm, him being on his own there and having everything to do himself.'

'That's a bit thick,' said Knell. 'When we first met him after Joss died, he was acting as though he was in sole charge of the family affairs. He could find time to spend the morning at Close-e-Cass arguing with the people there and throwing his weight about.'

'What makes it all the more funny is that before Joss came home and got himself killed, Sydney was never away from this place. It all started after he'd been to London to see Joss in prison. I think perhaps Joss asked him to keep an eye on me. I don't know why. Syd said he didn't like the idea of me being on my own. He even offered to take me in at his farm. As though I hadn't been alone here for most part of my life. He's a queer man and I don't know how our Rose puts up with him.'

'What did he do before he took to farming?'

'He was in the army when he met and married our Rose. Before that, I believe he lived with his mother and helped her with a shop near Stockport in England. He used to say they dealt in antiques, but our Joss always said they kept a junk shop, buying and selling old rubbish.'

They thanked her and left her to arrange her washing on the lines again, and made for Narradale. As they approached an acute corner of the steep winding road, a bell clanged furiously and Knell drew in to the side. An ambulance pulled up beside them and Kincaid, sitting beside the driver, thrust his honest, healthy face through the window.

'Sorry, we can't stay. We've got Sydney Handy inside. He's had an accident. Some sacks of oats fell on him from the loft. I think his back's broke. He'll be lucky if he's alive when we get to the cottage hospital.'

He addressed Knell.

'The representative from the corn merchants, Kinnish, found him. He must have been lying there for quite a while. I left Kinnish holding the fort. I've not looked over the place, sir. Would you mind...? Just until we can get him to Ramsey...'

The Archdeacon offered to sit with the injured man and the attendants seemed glad of it. Sydney Handy was dead when they arrived at their destination.

Littlejohn and Knell found the bewildered Kinnish waiting for relief in the gateway. P.C. Kincaid had told him as he left to touch nothing.

He was doing his best, walking up and down in the shabby unkempt farmyard, smoking one cigarette after another. A small, dark, middle-aged man, normally professionally pleasant and persuasive, now out of his depth and eager to share his worries with someone else. Attached to the farmhouse was a dilapidated stone barn, with an outside flight of stone steps mounting to a loft with a loading doorway on the first floor, over which hung a primitive derrick. In the yard directly below, a small heap of sacks filled with oats. Kinnish pointed to this even before he had greeted the newcomers.

'Those fell on him. He must have been lowering them from the loft, lost his footing and they fell down on him when he released the rope. I found him. I don't know how long he'd been there. He was unconscious and in bad shape. I had to move the sacks but it wasn't any use. I drove down for P.C. Kincaid. There's no 'phone here...'

He seemed relieved after unburdening himself of this information and Knell produced a small bottle of brandy from somewhere in the car and gave him a drink from it.

'Will you need me any more?'

'Not at present. We know where to find you, Mr. Kinnish. I'll get in touch.'

Knell gave him a friendly pat on the shoulder and saw him to his little car. Kinnish left them, driving at a slow respectful pace, as though he were already in the funeral procession.

There was an ominous silence about the place, punctuated now and then by the lamentations of the hens scratching about the yard and the snarling of the savage dog chained to his kennel. The shabbiness of the farm and its outbuildings contrasted sharply with the grandeur of the surrounding hills, with cattle grazing on the slopes. There was an atmosphere of melancholy and defeat about the whole set-up. Akin to Close Dhoo and the scene of as savage a climax.

Littlejohn and Knell wandered about the place as they waited for the return of Kincaid. They climbed into the loft whence Handy had apparently fallen. It contained a few sacks of oats and meal.

'I wonder what he was going to do for winter feed,' said Knell. 'There's not enough to last here until the end of the month. Handy must have been on his beam ends by the looks of things.'

The place was dirty and dust from the provender lay everywhere; much of it was trodden hard on the floor and it was impossible to trace footsteps in it. Littlejohn examined the derrick and the remaining bags in the loft. Then he looked down from the open door above the yard to the scattered pile of four bags which presumably had fallen on Handy.

'This is a simple derrick, Knell. At a guess I'd think it was adequate for lowering a couple of bags. Any more and it would get completely out of control and the load would crash to the ground below. You might just as well fling the bags down without using the crane. The same would apply if you were hoisting them up into the loft. Two bags would be as much as one man could cope with on a primitive affair like this.'

'And Handy was handling four...'

'He was presumably lowering them for use below. Otherwise, if he was hoisting them to the loft for storage there'd probably be some vehicle below from which he was removing them. There's no vehicle there. If he was lowering four bags with the help of that contraption they'd reach the ground, out of control, before he did, assuming he slipped and fell down. Kinnish found him *under* the bags.'

'Do you think someone else was here and arranged what he thought was an ingenious murder?'

'I don't know yet, Knell. But Sydney Handy has become a more important character in the Close Dhoo affair than we thought at first. He was obviously on the verge of bankruptcy, bitter, and almost out of his mind with worry. He, too, was the only member of the family – in fact, with the exception of Sarah Duffy, he was the only outsider – to visit Joss Varran in gaol. Joss sent for him. Why? The answer to that question might give us a lot of help.'

'Perhaps his wife knows.'

'I wish Kincaid would hurry and relieve us. We've a lot on our hands. We ought to be talking with quite a lot of people again on the strength of our morning's work. The Colonel, Sarah Duffy, Quantrell and now Mrs. Handy.'

Distant sounds of a hard pressed car climbing the hilly road, and then Kincaid arrived with another constable to relieve Littlejohn and Knell.

Kincaid didn't ask any questions, but simply reported that Handy had died on his way to hospital.

'He was unconscious all the time and never spoke a word. I met Kinnish, the commercial traveller who found Handy, on my way back here. He stopped to tell me you were waiting for me. I asked him if he'd passed anybody on his way to Handy's place but he said he hadn't. He didn't see a soul all the way up after he left Ginger Hall on the main road.'

'Is there another way here besides the main road?'

Kincaid rubbed his chin.

'There *is*, but I wouldn't like to try it in a car. It's one of what we call the back roads. It gave access to some old crofts, long neglected and ruined now, and I doubt if anybody ever uses it these days. The last time I was there, about some lost sheep, was around three years ago. It was rough and overgrown then. I don't know what it will be like now. In any case, it doesn't lead here. You have to walk about a mile across rough ground and there's a stream to cross. It's wild country. They call it the Park-ny-Earkan district...'

'Did you advise Douglas of this affair?'

'Yes, sir. I thought you'd wish that. They said they'd send out the technical squad right away, Inspector.'

'You did right. We're going back to the village now. Tell the men when they arrive to follow the usual procedure, but to treat this as a murder case. We're not saying it *is* murder, but as it's connected with the Close Dhoo affair we can't be too careful...And, by the way, tell them to take a look at that back road and particularly for traces of a vehicle or footprints.'

'Yes, sir.'

'We are going to the manor to see Colonel Duffy. If you want us urgently, you'll probably find us there within the next hour. If not, please report to us at your office. We'll call around three o'clock if we haven't seen you before. Have you been able to contact Mrs. Handy, by the way? Her sister said she was in Ramsey arranging about Joss's funeral tomorrow.'

'Yes. We called at Close Dhoo on the way back and found her there with her sister. The Archdeacon broke the news to her and she was for going to the cottage hospital right away. But Miss Isabel and the Archdeacon persuaded her there was nothing she could do there, as Syd was dead and she's staying with Isabel for the time being. I left the Archdeacon there.'

'We'd better call at Close Dhoo, then,' said Littlejohn.

They found Rose Handy there. She was obviously stricken, but an undemonstrative woman who kept her grief to herself and held her feelings well in check. She was dressed in black from head to foot for Joss. A more energetic woman than her sister, thick-set and stout, with the asthmatic voice and cyanosed cheeks of a heart patient. No doubt her life with Handy, living on the edge of ruin and subject to his ill-temper and bullying, had worn her out.

Knell and Littlejohn expressed their sympathy. Helped by the Archdeacon's presence there she had not given way to her shock and grief and was quite lucid.

'I don't understand what happened. The policeman said some bags of oats had fallen on him in the haggart from the loft and killed him...'

She used the old Manx word for farmyard, the haggart, and spoke in the lilting intonation of the older natives.

'What was he doing with sacks of corn falling on him?'

'There were four of them down in the yard, as though he'd been lowering them on the derrick.'

'But he wouldn't have been handling four at once. He used one at a time and dragged it to the door and dropped it down. He didn't use the crane. As for four... He'd never do that. He had a rupture and was always careful about lifting. What made him do that with four...?'

'We'll have to find out.'

'Do you feel able to answer one or two questions, Mrs. Handy?' asked Littlejohn.

'I'll try. Although the shock of it all has made me mixed up in my mind. Why did he do it? He'd never have...'

'Has he seemed strange lately?'

'Yes. He was proper upset about Joss. He got morose and couldn't sleep at night through thinkin' of it. But, if you think it would make him do away with himself, you're mistaken. He wasn't that sort. He was just worried, temporary like, and would have got over it.'

'Has anybody visited him lately?'

'No. Only the police since Joss's death.'

'You're sure?'

'I've always been at home. Except, there was Joss's death and funeral to see to. I've had more experience of such things than Isabel, so I went to Ramsey two or three times. Syd might have had callers while I was away. He didn't say.'

'Was he at home all night at the time of Joss's death?'

Mrs. Handy paused and then suddenly began to weep. Hard, bitter sobs which convulsed the whole of her body. Her sister rose alarmed, crossed to where she was sitting and put her arms round her. She looked at Littlejohn reproachfully.

'Can't you see she's beside herself and isn't fit to be worried with questions?'

Rose disentangled herself from Isabel's embrace.

'No, I can manage. It only struck me as strange that I can now say anything I like without Syd telling me to be quiet. You asked if he was at home the night Joss died. He wasn't, and he told me if I was asked, I'd to say he was.'

'Where did he go and at what time?'

'He went off in the van at two o'clock and didn't get back till about eleven at night. He said he was going to a farmers' meeting in Ramsey. I thought it funny, as he'd never been to the likes before. He wasn't a sociable man and hated meetings and things. I asked him when he got home if he'd seen our Joss and he flew in a temper and said he hadn't and it was no business of mine what he'd been doing.'

'Did you know when Joss expected to be back?'

'Joss never wrote to tell us when he was coming. I thought Syd might know, him having visited Joss, but when I asked him, he flew in such a rage that I never mentioned it to him again. So, I took it upon myself to ask the vicar if he could make some enquiries for me. Which he did by telephoning the prison chaplain. That's how we got to know the day he was released and when to expect Joss.'

'Your husband knew that?'

'No. I daren't tell him and I asked the vicar not to tell anybody.'

'You said nobody visited the farm between the death of Joss and that of your husband?'

'Yes.'

'Could the rag-and-bone man have called in your absence?'

'Cojeen the Rags, you mean? It's funny you should mention that. When I heard our Joss was dead I went down to see Isabel right away. When I left home there was a pile of old iron from some old machines in the haggart. Syd had kept saying he'd sell it for scrap, but never did anything. When I got back the old iron had gone. I asked him if Cojeen had been and he said no, and got in one of his usual rages and asked what it had got to do with me anyway.'

Knell gave Littlejohn an admiring look as the picture began to take shape in his mind. Cojeen the Rags; Cojeen the Liar!

'Just one more question, Mrs. Handy, if you don't mind...'

'I don't mind, sir, if it'll help you.'

'During the first year of his imprisonment, Joss wrote to your husband and asked him to visit him in gaol. What was it all about?'

'I don't know. I wish I did. He'd tell neither Isabel nor me a proper tale about it. All he'd say was that Joss seemed a bit homesick and wanted to see somebody from his family and get all the news of the Isle of Man. We never got to the bottom of why Sydney went. But he never seemed quite the same after it. Whether it was seeing what went on inside prison, or the sight of our Joss in his cell or among a lot of convicts turned his mind a bit, I don't know. He was moody and one minute saying better times were round the corner and the next down in the dumps. He was hard to live with, though I shouldn't say it.'

Littlejohn thanked her and they all prepared to take their leave.

'I'd like a word with Cojeen the Rags. I wonder where we can find him; I guess he's wandering all over the Island.'

'Not today,' said Isabel. 'There's a farm sale at Ballajack, Ballaugh. He's sure to be there waiting to pick up the odds and ends that nobody wants.'

They found Cojeen and Bessie, his little donkey, at Ballajack farm among a crowd of farmers, most of them dressed in their best, bidding with crafty diffidence as though they didn't care whether or not they'd secure the lots they'd set their hearts on. Knell sorted out Cojeen and took him aside, like a good sheep-dog cutting out a solitary sheep from the flock. This intrusion of the police in the middle of a murder case distracted interest in the auction, and one or two of the more cunning in the group secured bargains whilst the bidding flagged.

'The Chief Superintendent wants to ask you a question, Cojeen. Come along.'

'Me? Always glad to be of assistance to the law. Lead me to him.'

He greeted Littlejohn and the Archdeacon like old friends and the smile didn't even leave his crafty face when Littlejohn asked him:

'Why did you tell us that you saw Joss Varran being picked up by an old Bentley car on the night he returned here, when all the time it was Syd Handy's old van?'

'I'm certain I told you nothing of the kind, sir. I said I deduced it was a Bentley, not that I was sure. Facts are facts and deductions are deductions. One is proved, the other needs proving, sir.'

'Don't bandy words with me, Mr. Cojeen. After you saw Handy pick up Varran and then heard Varran had been killed, you thought you'd got a fine chance to squeeze Handy in exchange for your silence. He paid you well not only to keep quiet about seeing him, but also to say it was an old vintage Bentley that gave him the lift...'

'He told you that, did he? The ungrateful rascal. That's what he is. An ungrateful rascal. To ask a man to do a good turn and then to report him to the police. I committed no crime. I just helped what I thought was a friend. He swore to me that he hadn't anything to do with Joss's death, but that if the police got to hear that he was with Joss that night, they'd suspect him. It's no crime to ... '

'He didn't report it to the police.'

'How do you know, then?'

'Deductions,' said Littlejohn. 'Sydney Handy died this morning. He was murdered.'

It was then that Bessie brayed hoarsely. It sounded like a hearty laugh.

Chapter XI
The Game Bag

Quantrell was pottering about the grounds of Ballakee Manor when the. police arrived there. There was a motor cycle leaning against the garage, through the open doors of which they could see the vintage car, bright with brass. Now, after Cojeen's story, it seemed to have little importance in the present case.

As soon as he spotted them, Quantrell approached them. He had a sporting gun in his hand and a game-bag with a rabbit's head dangling from it over his arm. He looked dishevelled and unwashed as usual and his lips were scarlet against the thick black beard which obscured most of his face.

'You wanting me?'

'Among others, yes. We'd like to see the Colonel first.'

'You'll not be welcome at this time o' day. He's not at his best in the mornings.'

Littlejohn didn't seem to be listening.

'Tell the Colonel we're here and wish to see him, and you stay around. We'll need you later.'

'I'm not likely to run away. I'm here all day today.'

He walked in through the front door in his dirty boots and then returned.

'Is it important?'

'Of course it is. Why do you think we've traipsed out here?'

'He'll see you, then.'

'Is Miss Duffy at home?'

'She's cooking the dinner. She won't like it if she's disturbed.'

The Archdeacon remained outside in the car. Littlejohn went back and asked him to keep an eye on Quantrell and if he made any signs of departure to signal to him through the window.

Quantrell waited and then gave an impudent jerk of his head to indicate they could follow him and left them to enter and close the front door themselves. Without knocking, he opened a door to the left and waved them inside. Then he went out without another word.

Duffy was stretched in the large club chair with his feet on a stool. He did not rise to meet them. He gave Littlejohn a quick nod and ignored Knell.

'You here again. What do you want this time?'

He had changed in the short time since last they saw him. His complexion was yellow and there were dark shadows under his eyes. He had a look of general lethargy about him. He had, from all appearances, been drinking heavily.

'Some further information about the Varran case ... '

'You're wasting your time. I told you all I know when you called before. I hope you're not going to be long.'

'That depends on you, sir.'

'What do you mean by that?'

'Whether or not you give us some straight answers to our questions.'

'You'd better both sit down then. Looking up at you standing there gives me a crick in the neck.'

Littlejohn and Knell drew up chairs, one on either side of him with their backs to the window and the light falling full on the reclining man.

They had hardly settled themselves before the Archdeacon tapped on the window. He indicated with his forefinger that something was afoot farther along the front of the house. Littlejohn opened the window and leaned out. Quantrell, his game-bag and his gun on his back, had wheeled out his motor cycle and was starting it up.

'Quantrell! The Colonel wishes to see you...'

Duffy made no move to rise, but his face grew livid.

'What do you mean? I told him he could go and I don't...'

'Will you please be quiet. You *will* need him before we go.'

Quantrell hesitated.

'Come in here, Quantrell, if you don't wish me to come for you.'

The man leaned his motor cycle against the wall again and disappeared in the direction of the garage. When he returned he was without his game-bag, but still carried his gun.

'Leave the gun in the hall, Quantrell,' said Littlejohn.

Quantrell showed his teeth through his beard and was about to argue.

Duffy lost patience.

'Put the damned thing in the hall, Quantrell, and let's get on with this and rid ourselves of our callers. I'm supposed to be resting.'

Quantrell clumped out to the hall, returned without the gun and then without waiting for permission, drew up a chair and joined the group.

'And now, sir, would you mind sending for Miss Duffy?'

Duffy flew into a temper again.

'I'll be damned if I will. She's cooking in the kitchen and I don't see how including her in this jamboree will do any good.'

'Unless you send for her, sir, we will have to ask the three of you to accompany us to the police station and answer questions there.'

'And if we refuse to come?'

'We'll arrest the lot of you!'

Knell gave Littlejohn a quick look, wondering if the Colonel would challenge such a statement. Instead Duffy gave in.

'Oh, all right. Get her, Quantrell. If the lunch is spoiled she can blame it on the police.'

Quantrell shambled out as though he'd all the time in the world and they could hear his heavy boots crossing the hall. There was a pause and then he and Sarah Duffy sounded to emerge from somewhere in the back of the house and enter the hall, shouting all the way angrily, interrupting one another until finally they reached the door of the room and Quantrell flung it open.

She was in a furious rage, probably at having to leave her work, and was unsuccessfully trying to take it out on Quantrell. She might as well have beaten her head against the wall. He assumed a stupid oafish manner, now and then flinging back an impudent answer. His general attitude was one of somehow possessing a hold over the Duffys which he could use when he thought fit.

Sarah Duffy was wearing a long white coat for her kitchen work. It did not show her to the best advantage. Neutral white was a poor background for her flamboyant beauty. Duffy did not even look up to greet her.

Outside, the Archdeacon was visible through the window. He had laid aside the book he'd been reading and was now wandering round the unkempt front garden. Soon, he strolled out of sight, presumably into the wilderness behind. The sight of it seemed to upset Quantrell.

'What's the parson nosing about at? I like his cheek trespassing among other people's private property. I've a mind to go and tell him...'

Littlejohn turned on him.

'Leave the Archdeacon out of this, Quantrell, and be quiet. You'll stay here until I say you can go. Otherwise, we'll all adjourn to the local police station for our questions...'

Sarah Duffy, scarlet with anger, broke in, raising her voice to a shout to make herself heard.

'Will somebody tell me what all this is about? What are these policemen doing here again?'

Duffy looked at her over his shoulder.

'Better ask them. They haven't told me yet.'

'Please sit down, Miss Duffy. This may last quite a long time. I've a lot of questions to ask you all. But first let me give you some information. Sydney Handy died on his way to Ramsey cottage hospital an hour ago. He'd been murdered.'

There was a pause and then Duffy seemed to think he'd better say something.

'Who's Sydney Handy?'

'Surely you aren't telling me you don't know him. He was the brother-in-law of Joss Varran, and he seems to have got himself mixed up in the sorry business which has now led to both their deaths. But that's not all the story. It begins with the call here of Mr. Williams, the manager of Housmans Bank in Preston...'

Sarah Duffy rose quickly to her feet.

'I've no time to listen to your telling stories, Mr. Littlejohn. I've the lunch to prepare and it's spoiling in the oven ... '

'Please sit down, Miss Duffy. This concerns you as much as the rest of us. As I've said before, if our business is not completed here, it will be done at the police station. You may take your choice.'

She looked ready to resist further and then curiosity seemed to get the better of her.

'What is it all about then? I don't see ... '

'It is about the murder of Joss Varran. I'm trying to tell you how it occurred if you'll listen. It began with the visit of Mr. Williams. His bank, including the strongroom, was being rebuilt and the large door of the strongroom had not been delivered to time. This made it necessary, the old strong-room having been demolished, for the cash and securities to be kept temporarily in smaller safes, quite secure, Mr. Williams thought, but without the protection of the door of the vault. Two men were placed there on guard, therefore, every night after the staff left.'

Quantrell uttered a great and noisy yawn and stretched out his legs as though settling down to a little nap.

'You're not interested, Quantrell. You will be soon.'

Quantrell gave him an impudent pained look.

'It's most interesting, but what has it to do with me?'

'I'd have thought that an expert on safes like you would have been all ears.'

'Me? Safes?'

'You forget that the dinner is spoiling. Let me get on. Mr. Williams, an old neighbour of Colonel Duffy when they both lived in Preston, arrived on the Island on a holiday, called here sociably, and gave the Colonel all the details of the troubles the rebuilding was causing him. He also seems to have complained about the confusion due to the delayed delivery of the strong-room door. Colonel Duffy listened with great interest and I imagine before Mr. Williams had even said good-bye, he had started to hatch a plot to relieve him of some of his cash.'

Duffy choked and tried to get up. Then he was seized with a fit of coughing and sank back. Neither Sarah nor Quantrell offered him any help. He managed to utter a few words amid his paroxysms.

'If you're trying to involve me in the Preston bank robbery, you're making a mistake. I've not been near Preston since I moved to this place. My heart's too dicky for me even to walk to the end of the drive. Ask Sarah...'

'I'm not saying you robbed the bank. You merely planned the affair and left the job to others. Three of them...'

'You haven't a shred of proof. You're making up a fantastic tale to justify your intrusion here.'

'I was saying, there were three of them. Quantrell; Joss Varran; and you, Miss Duffy.'

Suddenly the three of them, Quantrell, the Colonel and Sarah Duffy were all shouting at once. Quantrell uttering a string of abuse and flat denials, Sarah trying to make them hear her say that she and the Colonel were at the manor on the night of the robbery and could prove it, and Duffy struggling to make himself heard and shouting incoherently.

Whilst all this was going on, P.C. Kincaid suddenly arrived in his van, got out and hurriedly sought out and spoke to the Archdeacon, who was still exploring the garden, and who with a wave of his hand, indicated where Littlejohn and Knell were. Littlejohn opened the window and spoke to Kincaid.

'Are you wanting to see me, Kincaid?'

'Will you excuse me a minute, sir...'

Kincaid had spotted Quantrell's old motor cycle leaning against the wall and made for it. He took a sheet of paper from his pocket and started to examine the tyres of the bike. Then he returned.

'We have been and explored the back road to Handy's farm, sir. It is in very bad condition and has been trampled by cattle. There are traces of motor cycle tyres going part of the way up towards Handy's, but the machine seems to have been parked about a mile from the farm and the rider must have walked the rest. There are signs of parking the cycle in the hedge, but no footprints, because the remainder lies across grass. I took a rough drawing of the impressions of the bike tyres and, in my opinion, which our experts can check later, they tally with those of the machine resting there against the wall.'

And he indicated Quantrell's old bike.

'Thanks, Kincaid. That will be of great help. Stay around. I'm just asking some more questions of Colonel Duffy and his friends.'

Littlejohn returned to the fray indoors and closed the window. The fracas had died away meanwhile, as the three participants had quietened to listen to what was going on at the window. They hadn't heard much, judging from their expressions.

'What's all that about?' asked Duffy.

He helped himself to more whisky from the bottle on the nearby table.

'I'll perhaps know better if I ask Quantrell a question ... '

Littlejohn turned to Quantrell who had taken out a pipe and started to smoke without even asking permission.

'What were you doing at Handy's farm this morning, Quantrell?'

'I wasn't there. Who says I was?'

'You went part of the way on your motor cycle. You left impressions of the tyres. The rest of the way, you walked ... '

'You're wrong. That was several days ago.'

'It rained last night. Now answer the question.'

'I repeat, I haven't been there for days.'

Littlejohn glanced at the Duffys. The expression on both their faces was uneasy, almost haggard, as though they were hanging now on the questions and answers which were piling up. They obviously wondered exactly how much Littlejohn knew.

'Very well, we'll come back to that later. I was outlining what happened prior to Varran's death. I said there were three people involved in the Preston bank robbery. Varran, whom you knew quite well, Colonel, in spite of the fact that you pretended you didn't when last we called. You needn't waste time by arguing. We have proof of it. The second was Quantrell ... '

Quantrell leaned forward to shout a challenge, but Littlejohn got in first.

'And don't you waste time, Quantrell, by further argument. We are sure of that, too. It needed an expert safe breaker and you were the man for the job. The Colonel knew that you and Varran were a couple of rascals to whom the easy money would be a temptation neither of you could resist. The third one of the party ... '

He paused and looked at Sarah Duffy. Her eyes were bright and challenging, as though she was eager to hear what was next.

'The third one was you, Miss Duffy.'

She made a strange guttural noise supposed to be a scornful laugh and rose.

'I never heard anything so fantastic in my life. You must be mad to think we'll believe such a tale. I'm going to finish off the lunch ... '

'Sit down, Miss Sarah Heron!'

She looked at Littlejohn incredulously. She was used to calling the tune and this was something new. And though she didn't protest at the use of her real name, she was momentarily startled at the extent of Littlejohn's knowledge of her.

She remained standing, but had obviously forgotten about the meal.

'Yes, it was you, Miss Duffy. It's easier to call you by that name. The Colonel was hardly likely to leave the whole exercise in the sole hands of a couple of the biggest scoundrels he knew. As he was unfit to travel – and if he was in his present condition on the night of the crime, I believe him – you had to be there to keep an eye on the loot. His precautions were in vain. You were disturbed half-way through the job, had to run for it, and Varran broke away with the money and joined the *Mary Peters* and away before you quite knew what he was up to.'

It was Duffy's turn to laugh this time. He made a croaking noise for he didn't seem to have enough breath to do anything else.

'That's an entertaining tale, Littlejohn, but not a word of it's true.'

'We'll see. Quantrell and Miss Duffy soon decided what Varran had done and the chase, which lasted until the night of Varran's death, commenced. They couldn't reach the Isle of Man before him. The *Mary Peters* sailed almost as soon as he boarded her and Varran was at Close Dhoo before the first available boat or plane left for the Island. By the time they arrived here, Varran had hidden the money and was safely back aboard his ship, where the pair of you couldn't get at him. He knew that unless he could evade you, get his hidden money back and disappear, it wouldn't pay him to be alone again...'

Sarah Duffy reached for a cigarette from a box on the table and lit it calmly.

'In this tale you're telling, there seems to be one flaw. Why did Varran flee to the Isle of Man? He knew the others would follow him there. Why didn't he remain in England where he'd more scope for hiding?'

'As soon as the three of you were disturbed, Varran was on the run not only from the pair of you, but from the police. He was in a hurry and sought the best hiding place he knew, his ship. But in his panic, he forgot that once at sea, he was trapped. He had to go to the Isle of Man, because the *Mary Peters* was bound for it and, short of diving overboard, there he must go, too. He'd just time to hide his money and get back to his ship and then he found you'd both arrived and were on his trail. He remained, safe among his shipmates, until he got to London. The two of you had followed him there, and soon he'd have to face the music. He couldn't remain aboard the *Mary Peters* for ever. He was a violent impulsive man when cornered and chose a novel way of shaking you off until the heat subsided. He decided to spend a cooling-off period in gaol. As I said, he was impulsive, but rather short of brains and that caused his downfall and his death.'

Strangely enough, none of them interrupted him this time. Littlejohn wondered whether his theory was proving true in every detail, or else the Duffys and Quantrell were amazed at his mastery of the fabulous.

'Whilst he was in gaol, two people called to see him. Miss Duffy and his brother-in-law, Sydney Handy. Varran refused to see Miss Duffy. He knew that she'd either called to make a deal or else to threaten him if he didn't play along with her and her associates. Handy paid Varran a visit because Varran had asked him to do so. Both are dead and we'll never know what happened in that interview. I imagine he asked his brother-in-law to keep an eye on Close Dhoo and perhaps he even obliquely mentioned the money he had hidden. Such information would doubtless have corrupted Handy, a greedy bitter man whose failure in life had made him quite unscrupulous and willing to do anything to reverse his run of bad luck.'

For some reason, Quantrell seemed to think it was his turn to speak.

'We all know what sort of a man Handy was. What has he to do with what you're telling us about the bank raid?'

Duffy jerked up his head in alarm, as though fearing that if Quantrell started to talk he'd involve the three of them in disaster.

'Shut up, Quantrell! Nobody asked you to put in your motto. The sooner the Superintendent finishes this rigmarole, the sooner I'll get my lunch. It's well past the time.'

Littlejohn looked through the window. The Archdeacon had reappeared from wherever he'd been spending his time and was sitting in the car again, with P.C. Kincaid watching him through the open window. The Archdeacon seemed to be writing and then handed Kincaid a note which Kincaid carried to the front door of the house.

The bell rang and Quantrell made as if to answer it.

'Wait, Quantrell. I'll attend to that.'

Quantrell shrugged his shoulders and gave place to Littlejohn.

Kincaid was obviously excited, but handed over his note without a word. Littlejohn read it and felt as excited as Kincaid, even if he didn't show it.

'Where was it?'

'Locked in a big wooden tool-box in the old vintage car in the garage. The Archdeacon searched the place. Quantrell must have hidden it there when you sent for him to join you. It was under the rabbit sticking out of the top of his game-bag.'

'Did the Archdeacon break the lock of the box?'

'No. He said he tried the keys on his key-ring and the one that locks the cupboard where he keeps the communion wine at the church did the trick.'

'Get the bag, please. And then join us indoors. We may need you.'

Kincaid went back and the Archdeacon passed the bag to him through the car window. Littlejohn waved congratulations to him. Then he returned to the waiting party. He held up the bag with the rabbit still hanging out.

'Quite a good morning's sport, Quantrell. One rabbit, Sydney Handy, and this...'

And before Quantrell could reach him, he inverted the game-bag over the table and shook out a shower of banknotes.

CHAPTER XII
ROGUES FALL OUT

Littlejohn returned to his seat and sat down and Kincaid took up an almost rigid position behind him, like a bodyguard.

The notes still lay in a confused pile on the table, just as they'd fallen there. Quantrell kept looking at them and licking his lips, which were like two red slits through his beard, as though he were waiting a chance to pick up the cash and bolt.

The Duffys were worried, but they tried to brazen out the situation.

'Well?'

Littlejohn said it hopefully, as though awaiting some good news.

'Well what?'

Quantrell asked the question, as if expecting Littlejohn to tell him to gather up the loot, take it with him, and clear off.

'Where's the rest? I suppose there's about five thousand pounds there on the table. Where's the rest? Your shares, Colonel and Miss Duffy? One thing seems in your favour, Quantrell. You were at least more honest than Varran. You returned to share the spoils; he tried to make off with the lot. Why did you do that?'

Quantrell swallowed hard. Caught in the net, he'd lost a lot of his self-confidence and cheek. He answered the question in a low voice which was almost smothered by his beard.

'I know from experience what Joss Varran didn't. That woman's a devil. She'll stop at nothing.'

Sarah Duffy's eyes narrowed.

'Just remember that, Quantrell, and tell no more lies to save your own skin. That's all. Watch it!' she said.

Littlejohn ignored the threats.

'You surely don't mean to tell me that trifle on the table was all you stole from the bank. Where's the rest you took from Sydney Handy before you killed him to silence him in case he came to us with his tale?'

'I don't know what you're talking about.'

'Let us refresh your memory, then. You were a very persevering couple in pursuit of your loot. You guessed that Varran had hidden the money somewhere on the Island during the brief time he'd spent here on the night you stole it and he got here a step ahead of you. You had only to spot him and tail him when he returned home from gaol. You daren't attack him or even allow yourselves to be seen. Otherwise he'd never have led you to his hiding-place. You found out when he was expected home, either from Handy, who Joss thought was the only one who knew the exact day of his return and who could never keep his mouth shut; or by enquiring from his associates in gaol who'd been released before him; or else from the gaol itself. That doesn't matter; you were there when he left the boat at Douglas.'

Duffy was thoroughly fed up. He was still drinking and reclining in his chair as though he hadn't even the energy to move or object to what was going on. His colour had gone

and he mustered just enough effort to reach for the whisky
bottle and pour himself a fresh drink. He gulped half of it
down and it seemed to brace him. He waved a limp hand
backwards and forwards.

'How much longer is this long rigmarole going on? It's
exhausting me. I'll be having another heart attack...'

'I won't take much more of your time, sir. And then you'll
be left to yourself for a while. I propose to take Quantrell
and Miss Duffy back with us to Ramsey, where they'll be
charged: Quantrell with the murder of Sydney Handy, and
Miss Duffy with the bank robbery at Preston. There will, I'm
sure, be other charges later, but that will be enough for the
time being.'

Quantrell leapt to his feet as though about to make a
fight of it, but Knell was ready and thrust him back in his
chair with a quick jerk.

'Watch it, Quantrell! The Chief hasn't finished yet.'

'If the two of us are being taken to the cooler, innocent
though we are and ready to prove it, what about him?'

Quantrell pointed a dirty forefinger at Duffy.

'He'll hold himself at our disposal and if he tries to run
away, we'll soon bring him back.'

Duffy laughed feebly.

'Run away, did you say? I couldn't run across the room
without dropping dead. I've got an aneurism and my number's up.'

This seemed to annoy Sarah Duffy more than the idea
of going to Ramsey to be charged. She had sat through
Littlejohn's statement with a confident sneer on her face,
but Duffy's pathetic effort infuriated her.

'Don't listen to him. He drinks too much, that's all.
Aneurism! He hasn't even been to a doctor. He's diagnosed

it from *Everybody's Home Doctor*. If anything's wrong with him it's his liver. Pickled in whisky.'

'This is no time for quarrelling among yourselves. You'll all be charged, including the colonel as accessory, before and after, to say the least of it. And now, if you'll allow me to continue. You were on Varran's trail as he left Douglas. He tried to shake you off by pursuing a roundabout course. We haven't been able to trace precisely the route he took; probably you were more successful. He ended his day in Ramsey and, at nine o'clock, was recognised by Cojeen, the ragman, drinking in a bar...'

Quantrell snorted.

'A fine witness. He's a well-known liar.'

'We're well aware of that. Cojeen put us off the trail by telling us that Varran was picked up on the quay by a car, an old Bentley, which turned our thoughts to Colonel Duffy...'

'That wasn't the first mistake you made, as you'll find out when you encounter our lawyer.'

'Actually, he was met by his brother-in-law in his van. Sydney Handy, after Varran's murder, was afraid he'd become involved if it was known that he had met Varran, as you'd already arranged with him, and was probably one of the last to see him alive. He knew Cojeen had spotted him, so quickly made a point of seeing him after the crime and bribing him to tell the police, if asked, that the Bentley car had given Varran a lift home. Why did he do that? Because he was, in fact, involved, to the extent of being paid to ascertain, by hook or crook, where the loot was hidden. We don't know how successfully he did his work of spying. Perhaps he took an opportunity of searching the house and grounds, but he didn't discover the hideout. He hadn't found out a thing, and at last Varran was back in Ramsey. Handy must have prowled about all day there, hoping to find Joss, offer him a lift and take him home, where presumably the other parties to the crime had been on the look-out most of the afternoon and evening. If the money was hidden outside, they'd look after it. If it was hidden somewhere inside the house, Handy, with his entree as a relative, hoped by hook or by crook to find out. Presumably his hirers had promised no harm would come to Joss. All they wanted was their shares. Instead, Handy's usual run of bad luck prevailed. Joss was in a hurry to get a spade, dig up the money and disappear. His pursuers hadn't shown themselves and he imagined he was safe...'

'Wait a minute!'

Quantrell seemed carried away by Littlejohn's description of events. His bloodshot eyes bulged.

'You've missed something out. Where was the money hid?'

'Shut your mouth, Quantrell! None of us is saying a word until we've our lawyer with us. This has gone too far. Before we know where we are, we'll find ourselves guilty of crimes we've not committed.'

Sarah Duffy was on hot coals. The story was moving too fast for her liking and, at any moment, she expected a climax. She rose hastily.

'I'm going. Lunch has already spoiled, I'm sure, but I'm going to rescue what I can and nobody's going to stop me...'

'Sit down, Miss Duffy. There's nothing much to follow... Only the end of the tale...'

Knell who had been watching her closely, suddenly pounced, grasped her hand and dragged it from the pocket of her coat. There was a brief struggle and Knell ended up holding a revolver, small, but very efficient looking. She must have gathered it up on her way to the interview.

'I could see the shape of it in the pocket of her coat,' explained Knell.

Duffy, by now, was drunk and didn't seem to know quite what was happening.

'Will somebody tell me what all this is about...?'

Quantrell made a move, too. He took a step towards the door and Kincaid seized him in an arm lock and forced him back in his chair.

'No use you making off for *your* gun. I've put it in the car outside.'

Sarah Duffy sat snorting on her chair like an angry tigress. Littlejohn felt that given a chance, she'd turn violent and fight it out.

'Well,' she said. 'Where is all this leading? You can't prove anything.'

'We know enough. Handy didn't drive Varran to the door of Close Dhoo, otherwise Isabel Varran would have heard his old rattle-trap of a van grinding along outside. Instead, Varran told Handy to put him down at the end of the road. Handy did so, but followed him quietly. Instead of entering the house, Varran called in the garden shed for a spade and made off to dig up his money from the neighbouring field, the Shaking Field...'

Littlejohn watched Quantrell as he was speaking and noticed that his forehead was covered with beads of sweat. The man didn't speak but a faint look of relief crossed his face as though he'd been told the answer to a riddle which had baffled him for long.

'I can tell from your face, Quantrell, that you didn't see the money being dug up. You and your companion lost him in the dark. I know you had a companion, because Varran was too formidable to tackle single-handed.'

Quantrell glanced interrogatively at Sarah Duffy who answered with a look of hatred. She was afraid he was going to give the show away in some way or another and didn't know how to stop him

'You came upon him as he was returning to Close Dhoo with his kit-bag crammed with banknotes, followed by Handy. It was like a game of hide-and-seek in the curraghs played with grim silence. So quietly, that even Varran's sister who was waiting for him didn't hear a sound. And you all found one another right opposite the house. Handy included, for you gave him a black eye and lamed him with kicks. He must have been suddenly transformed from a miserable coward into an angry and perhaps brave man by the sudden attack on his brother-in-law and he joined in the scrimmage. It didn't last long, because Handy in the scuffle came upon Varran's kit-bag, seized it and ran for his life and hid until it was all over. You struck Varran down, Quantrell, and left him to die in the ditch ... '

Quantrell leapt to his feet.

'I'm getting out of here!' he cried and made for the door before anyone could stop him. Kincaid caught him as he fumbled with the door handle, seized him by both shoulders and pinned him to the panelled wall with one knee. Quantrell struggled like a madman and foamed at the mouth. Knell rushed across and he and Kincaid dragged him back and flung him in his chair. All the time Quantrell continued to shout as he gulped in enough breath to do so. It was like a scene in a third-rate melodrama. Quantrell looking like a crazy Svengali with froth on his beard, Sarah Duffy transfixed and horror-struck waiting for what she knew would now, sooner or later, be said and not knowing what to do to avoid it. And Duffy himself, drunk as a lord, gabbling incoherently with drunken eloquence. Among the slurred words they heard him asking why nobody had told him what had happened on the night they killed Varran. Finally he couldn't even find his mouth in which to pour another drink and scattered the whisky all over himself.

Quantrell was beside himself with rage and fright.

'You're trying to pin another murder on me. Well, you're wrong. I never did. I didn't. I was on the ground trying to disentangle myself from Handy. He was nothing of a fighter, but he clung like a leech. Then all of a sudden, he jumped up and ran off like hell. When I got to my feet, she was groping about for the bag and Varran was lying dead in the ditch...'

'Liar! Liar! You know it was you who hit him. How could I...?'

Sarah Duffy suddenly came to life with a shout that was hair-raising. Knell had to hold her back for she went for Quantrell tooth and claw. Quantrell was so immersed that he didn't even rise to defend himself. He just continued to shout.

'Liar yourself! You hit him with the hunting crop you were carrying. It couldn't have been anything else. I didn't touch him. Handy clung to me like a madman, his arms and legs wrapped round me, scratching and biting...'

Littlejohn, the only one of the party not dishevelled, persisted in ending his tale, by which he had succeeded in breaking the resistance of the Duffy gang in a flurry of hysterical hatred and fear.

'Handy hid and he heard you both beating a retreat because Isabel had opened the door of Close Dhoo and you didn't know that she was waiting there alone. She found Joss, thought him dead, and went for help. And then Handy emerged from his hiding-place, found Varran and carried him in the house, where he tried to revive him. But Varran was dead by then and Handy had to make off and scuttered to his car and away to Narradale. It wasn't until the pair of you thought the heat was off that you dared approach Handy. Then, Quantrell made his way to Narradale to claim the money...'

Quantrell was seized by another frenzy.

'It was an accident. I didn't kill him...'

'You manhandled him until he told you where the money was. He'd hidden it in the loft and when you got it, you flung him down into the yard because he knew too much. And then you tried to engineer the appearance of an accident.'

Quantrell made one last effort to escape. He leapt from his chair and ran to the window as though intending to dive through it. As he moved, however, Duffy, for some reason, stretched out a leg and Quantrell fell full length. He lay there, swearing and foaming, until Knell lifted him by the scruff of his neck and bounced him to his feet. And then Sarah Duffy hit Quantrell with her fist right on the nose which started to bleed.

'Where is the rest of the money, Colonel?'

Littlejohn seemed relentlessly apart from the confusion ensuing.

'Eh?'

'The money. We will search the house if you don't tell us.'

'Oh, *that.*'

Duffy rose, clinging to the arms of the chair in support, turned and removed the cushion on which he'd been sitting all the time. The seat was old and sagged badly and in the cavity reposed Joss Varran's old kit-bag. Duffy fumbled drunkenly with the cord which closed the top of the bag and finally opened it. Then he inverted the bag and littered the rug with soiled pound and five pound notes.

'There you are. Take 'em.'

They took the three of them to gaol. They were charged with murder and convicted. The police found Sarah Duffy's heavy hunting-crop. It had been cleaned, but there were still traces of blood on it. Sarah was charged in her own name. Duffy's mistress. She was, at least, loyal to him. She didn't say a word against him. Quantrell did that. Duffy's aneurism turned out to be an ulcer, which they cured in prison and he was treated like the rest of them.

THE CASE OF THE FAMISHED

PARSON

GEORGE BELLAIRS

CHAPTER I
THE TOWER ROOM

Wednesday, September 4th. The Cape Mervin Hotel was as quiet as the grave. Everybody was "in" and the night-porter was reading in his cubby-hole under the stairs.

A little hunchbacked fellow was Fennick, with long arms, spindleshanks accentuated by tight, narrow-fitting trousers—somebody's cast-offs—and big feet. Some disease had robbed him of all his hair. He didn't need to shave and when he showed himself in public, he wore a wig. The latter was now lying on a chair, as though Fennick had scalped himself for relief.

The plainwood table was littered with papers and periodicals left behind by guests and rescued by the porter from the salvage dump. He spent a lot of his time reading and never remembered what he had read.

Two or three dailies, some illustrated weeklies of the cheaper variety, and a copy of Old Moore's Almanac. A sporting paper and a partly completed football pool form. ...

Fennick was reading "What the Stars have in Store." He was breathing hard and one side of his face was contorted with concentration. He gathered that the omens were favourable. Venus and Jupiter in good aspect. Success in love affairs and a promising career. ... He felt better for it.

Outside the tide was out. The boats in the river were aground. The light in the tower at the end of the breakwater changed from white to red and back at minute intervals. The wind blew up the gravel drive leading from the quayside to the hotel and tossed bits of paper and dead leaves about. Down below on the road to the breakwater you could see the coke glowing in a brazier and the silhouette of a watchman's cabin nearby.

The clock on the Jubilee Tower on the promenade across the river struck midnight. At this signal the grandfather clocks in the public rooms and hall began to chime all at once in appalling discord, like a peal of bells being 'fired.' The owner of the hotel was keen on antiques and bric-a-brac and meticulously oiled and regulated all his clocks himself.

Then, in mockery of the ponderous timepieces, a clock somewhere else cuckooed a dozen times. The under-manager, who had a sense of humour, kept it in his office, set to operate just after the heavy ones. Most people laughed at it. So far, the proprietor hadn't seen the point.

Fennick stirred himself, blinked his hairless eyelids, laid aside the oracle, stroked his naked head as though soothing it after absorbing so much of the future, and rose to lock the main door. Then he entered the bar.

The barmaid and cocktail-shaker had been gone almost an hour. Used glasses stood around waiting to be washed first thing in the morning. The night-porter took a tankard from a hook and emptied all the dregs from the glasses into it. Beer, stout, gin, whisky, vermouth. ... A good pint of it. ... One hand behind his back, he drank without stopping, his prominent Adam's-apple and dewlaps agitating, until it was all gone. Then he wiped his mouth on the back of his hand, sighed with satisfaction, selected and lighted the largest cigarette-end from one of the many ash-trays scattered about and went off to his next job.

It was the rule that Fennick collected all shoes, chalked their room-numbers on their soles and carried them to the basement for cleaning. But he had ways of his own. He took a large newspaper and his box of cleaning materials and silently dealt with the footwear, one by one, as it stood outside the doors of the bedrooms, spreading the paper to protect the carpet.

Fennick started for the first floor. Rooms 1, 2, 3, 4 and 5, with the best views over the river and bay. His gait was jaunty, for he had had a few beers before finally fuddling himself with the dregs from the bar. He hummed a tune to himself.

Don't send my boy to prizzen,
It's the first crime wot he's done. ...

He tottered up the main staircase with his cleaning-box and stopped at the first door.

Number I was a single room. Once it had been double, but the need for more bathrooms had split it in two. Outside, on the mat, a pair of substantial handmade black shoes. Fennick glided his two brushes and polishing-cloth over them with hasty approval. They belonged to Judge Tennant, of the High Court. He came every year at this time for a fishing holiday. He tipped meticulously. Neither too much not too little. Yet you didn't mind. You felt justice had been done when you got it.

Fennick had been sitting on his haunches. Now and then he cocked an ear to make sure that nobody was stirring. He moved like a crab to Number 2 gently dragging his tackle along with him.

This was the best room, with a private bath. Let to a millionaire, they said. It was a double, and in the register the occupants had gone down as Mr. and Mrs. Cuhady. All the staff, from the head waiter down to the handyman who raked the gravel round the hotel and washed down the cars, knew it was a lie. The head waiter was an expert on that sort of thing. With thirty years' experience in a dining-room you can soon size-up a situation.

That was how they knew about the honeymoon couple in Number 3, too. Outside their door was a pair of new men's brogues and some new brown suede ladies' shoes. "The Bride's travelling costume consisted of...with brown suede shoes...." Fennick knew all about it from reading his papers in the small hours.

There were five pairs of women's shoes outside Number 2. Brown leather, blue suede, black and red tops, light patent leather, and a pair with silk uppers. All expensive ones.

Five pairs in a day! Fennick snarled and showed a nasty gap where he had lost four teeth. Just like her! He cleaned the brown, the black-and-red and the patent uppers with the same brushes for spite. The blue suede he ignored altogether. And he spat contemptuously on the silk ones and wiped them with a dirty cloth.

Mr. Cuhady seemed to have forgotten his shoes altogether. That was a great relief! He was very particular about them. Lovely hand-made ones and the colour of old mahogany. And you had to do them properly, or he played merry hell. Mr. Cuhady had blood-pressure and "Mrs." Cuhady didn't seem to be doing it any good. The magnate was snoring his head off. There was no other sound in Number 2. Fennick bet himself that his partner was noiselessly rifling Cuhady's pocket-book....

He crawled along and dealt with the honeymoon shoes. They weren't too good. Probably they'd saved-up hard to have their first nights together at a posh hotel and would remember it all their lives. "Remember the Cape Mervin ...?" Fennick, sentimental under his mixed load of drinks, spat on all four soles for good luck ... He crept on.

Two pairs of brogues this time. Male and female. Good ones, too, and well cared for. Fennick handled them both with reverence. A right good job. For he had read a lot in his papers about one of the occupants of Room 4. An illustrated weekly had even interviewed him at Scotland Yard and printed his picture.

On the other side of the door were two beds, separated by a table on which stood a reading-lamp, a travelling-clock and two empty milk glasses. In one bed a good-looking, middle-aged woman was sitting-up, with a dressing-gown round her shoulders, reading a book about George Sand.

In the other a man was sleeping on his back. On his nose a pair of horn-rimmed spectacles; on the eiderdown a thriller had fallen from his limp hand. He wore striped silk pyjamas and his mouth was slightly open.

The woman rose, removed the man's glasses and book, drew the bedclothes over his arms, kissed him lightly on his thinning hair, and then climbed back into bed and resumed her reading. Inspector Littlejohn slept on ....

Fennick had reached the last room of the block. Number 5 was the tower room. The front of the Cape Mervin Hotel was like a castle. A wing, a tower, the main block, a second tower, and then another wing. Number 5 was in the left-hand tower. And it was occupied at the time by the Bishop of Greyle and his wife.

As a rule there were two pairs here, too. Heavy, brown serviceable shoes for Mrs. Bishop; boots, dusty, with solid, heavy soles and curled-up toes, for His Lordship. Tonight there was only one pair. Mrs. Greyle's. Nobody properly knew the bishop's surname. He signed everything "J. C. Greyle" and they didn't like to ask his real name. Somebody thought it was Macintosh.

Fennick was so immersed in his speculations that he didn't see the door open. Suddenly looking up he found Mrs. Greyle standing there in a blue dressing-gown staring down at him.

The night-porter hastily placed his hand flat on the top of his head to cover his nakedness, for he'd forgotten his wig. He felt to have a substantial thatch of hair now, however, and every hair of his head seemed to rise.

"Have you seen my husband?" said Mrs. Greyle, or Macintosh, or whatever it was. "He went out at eleven and hasn't returned."

Fennick writhed from his haunches to his knees and then to his feet, like a prizefighter who has been down.

"No, mum...I don't usually do the boots this way, but I'm so late, see?"

"Wherever can he be...? So unusual...."

She had a net over her grey hair. Her face was white and drawn. It must have been a very pretty face years ago.... Her hands trembled as she clutched her gown to her.

"Anything I can do, mum?"

"I can't see that there is. I don't know where he's gone. The telephone in our room rang at a quarter to eleven and he just said he had to go out and wouldn't be long. He didn't explain...."

"Oh, he'll be turnin' up. P'raps visitin' the sick, mum."

Fennick was eager to be off. The manager's quarters were just above and if he got roused and found out Fennick's little cleaning dodge, it would be, as the porter inwardly told himself, Napooh!

It was no different the following morning, when the hotel woke up. The bishop was still missing.

At nine o'clock things began to happen.

First, the millionaire sent for the manager and raised the roof.

His shoes were dirty. Last night he'd put them out as usual to be cleaned. This morning he had found them, not only uncleaned, but twice as dirty as he'd left them. In fact, muddy right up to the laces. He demanded an immediate personal interview with the proprietor. Somebody was going to get fired for it....

"Mrs." Cuhady, who liked to see other people being bullied and pushed around, watched with growing pride and satisfaction the magnate's mounting blood-pressure...

At nine-fifteen they took the bishop's corpse to the town morgue in the ambulance. He had been found at the bottom of Bolter's Hole, with the tide lapping round his emaciated body and his head bashed in.

The first that most of the guests knew of something unusual was the appearance of the proprietor in the dining-room just after nine. This was extraordinary, for Mr. Allain was a lazy man with a reputation for staying in bed until after ten.

Mr. Allain, a tall fat man and usually impurturbable, appeared unshaven and looking distracted. After a few words with the head waiter, who pointed out a man eating an omelette at a table near the window, he waddled across the room.

They only got bacon once a week at the Cape Mervin and Littlejohn was tackling an omelette without enthusiasm. His wife was reading a letter from her sister at Melton Mowbray who had just had another child.

Mr. Allain whispered to Littlejohn. All eyes in the room turned in their direction. Littlejohn emptied his mouth and could be seen mildly arguing. In response, Mr. Allain, who was half French, clasped his hands in entreaty. So, Littlejohn, after a word to his wife, left the room with the proprietor....

"Something must have happened," said the guests one to another.

Want another Perfect Mystery?

Get your next Classic Crime Story for FREE ...

Sign up to our Crime Classics newsletter where you can discover new Golden Age crime, receive exclusive content and never-before published short stories, all for FREE.

From the beloved greats of the golden age to the forgotten gems, best-kept-secrets, and brand new discoveries, we're devoted to classic crime.

If you sign up today, you'll get:

1. A Free Novel from our Classic Crime collection.
2. Exclusive insights into classic novels and their authors and the chance to get copies in advance of publication, and
3. The chance to win exclusive prizes in regular competitions.

Interested? It takes less than a minute to sign up. You can get your novel and your first newsletter by signing up on our website www.crimeclassics.co.uk